Whatever Happens

Whatever Happens

Tim Conley

implosion
imprint

INSOMNIAC PRESS

Library and Archives Canada Cataloguing in Publication

Conley, Tim, 1972-
 Whatever happens / Tim Conley.

Short stories.
ISBN 1-897178-13-1

I. Title.

PS8605.O56W43 2006   C813'.54   C2005-907630-5

The publisher gratefully acknowledges the support of the Canada Council, the Ontario Arts Council and the Department of Canadian Heritage through the Book Publishing Industry Development Program.

Printed and bound in Canada

Insomniac Press
192 Spadina Avenue, Suite 403,
Toronto, Ontario, Canada, M5T 2C2
www.insomniacpress.com

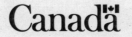

This book is for my friend
Raymond Lake

Contents

Means to an End

Knock-knock! How absurd, how disappointing, how vulgar was that sound at that moment. Looking from his quickly polished shoes up to the unlocked door and then again to the rope at eye-level, Maurice hoped his weight would not evince any creak of strain from the table. In all likelihood – a phrase he suddenly realized he despised – whoever it was would go away after a moment. It had been silence all day until – *knock-knock!* Again. Maurice tried to re-examine his mind's last checklist: shoes, teeth, curtains, letter. No letter yet, but of course that one was optional. Hard not to be reductive, or even corny, really. Everything else on the list had been gently taken care of, not counting the inevitable Qualms of the Last Minute, deliberately omitted from the list so as to pass them by with greater aplomb. *Knock-knock!* Louder. Better to answer than have the operation interrupted. The eyelash of difference between absurd and ignoble. That's a nice phrase, Maurice wished he'd used it in the letter but no, too late, right after this importunate visitor he would have done with it, letter or no.

Who is it?

A young woman's voice. In a voice greyed with sad frustration, she asked Maurice if he had any rope. Before he could lie, she went on to say that she was another tenant in the building, and that another tenant down the hall, Mme. Fouinarde, had told her when asked that by coincidence he, the monsieur in number three, had been seen bringing home a length of rope just that morning. Unable to think of a dodge to this, Maurice got down from the table and opened the door an uncompromising sliver. He had seen her before: pretty, in a plain and unaffected sort of way, but absent, *une distraite*.

As a matter of fact, he said, assuming a diplomatic tone, I do have some rope. But just now it's in use, you see.

Oh, but I only want to borrow a length of it. I don't need very much and you will get it back quickly.

He asked whether he could give her the rope the next day, or even in a couple of hours, but no, no, her need was urgent, and she again assured him of its return. Yet despite her insistence, Maurice sensed a bluff which he was very coyly and perhaps even unconsciously being invited to call. The rope's not very good, he told her. Surely that depends on what it's used for, she countered. What *are* you going to use it for? he asked. A good change of tactic, but still she outmaneuvered him: Nothing you'd be interested in, she said, and before he could reply added, Well? Can I borrow some rope or not?

Hold on a moment, he said, and closed the door. What was it, between the ignoble and the absurd, he'd forgotten, but that was out the window now. He remounted the table and, with a little difficulty, unworked the knot he had carefully wound above him. Life meant having neighbours, he said to himself, and turned it into a silent mantra. He brought the rope to the door and, before putting it into the young woman's eager hands, asked: Not long, you said? And, giving her the bundled rope, continued, I'll just wait here in the hall.

I can just as easily bring it to you.

Oh, it's no bother. I was just using it and need it back for what I'm doing.

She gave him a studying look and turned to walk to her door, number five. The door closed behind her and, yes, locked.

Standing there in the hall, Maurice was strangely put in mind of the time lightning had struck an electrical pole in front of an apartment he'd been living in for some time. Cleaved it neatly in two at the top, left it standing there unobserved like a tall letter Y and Maurice without dial tone for two days. Something about nearly getting blasted himself had bewildered and excited him and at least twice he had scooped up the telephone to tell someone before registering the silence of defeat. He was smiling like an idiot thinking, how do you express that you can't express? when M. Gênant drifted into the hallway.

Unlike most people, whose heads can be discerned from the bodies and limbs from torso, M. Gênant was all of one piece. Though shaped like the crudest snowman, he moved in such a graceful and silent way that he seemed to hover just above the floor and glide to this place or that. But his most alarming feature, which he now presented, was his arsenal of small talk from which no passerby was safe. He examined Maurice's opinion on the weather, shifted to notice of the one creaking stair that had not been fixed, made a general observation on the inconveniences of apartment living, and by the time he arrived at explaining his recently revised holiday plans by way of updating his listener who heretofore only knew of the original and rather preliminary plans, Maurice was becoming very nervous about his rope.

Pardon me, he said, and turned to give loud knocks to the young woman's door.

M. Gênant theatrically lowered his voice and confided that the young woman did keep to herself, very quiet, but pretty, yes, undoubtedly, a musician, you know, though quiet, reserved and quiet herself, one wonders what she's thinking.

Maurice knocked again, louder this time. *Knock-knock!*

I've always wondered when they're going to bother putting buzzers or bells in, sighed M. Gênant. It's not as though it would cost very much and (*knock-knock!*) the noise factor in the building would be cut down considerably (*knock-knock!*), not that that's such a great problem here at present (*knock-knock!*), but you never (*knock-knock-knock!*)...

The young woman opened the door suddenly, but only slightly.

Yes? she had the nerve to say.

I want my rope back now, said Maurice.

Perhaps sensing that the conversation now extended beyond the superficial, M. Gênant floated away, enigmatically remarking as he went that rope was something he'd always meant to investigate for himself.

It's just barely long enough, she said.

Maurice could not decide if this was an insult or another interrogation technique, but it remained for him to ask: Long enough for what?

She shrugged. I suppose I can use it after you're done with it, if you're in a hurry and you'll be done quickly.

He protested that he wasn't certain how quickly he would be finished with the rope. She expressed her concern that she might put too much strain on it and he would find it too damaged for his use afterwards, so it might be best for him to finish with it before she set to work with it. He doubted that the strain she intended to put on the rope exceeded what he was going to use it for, and noted that it was strong rope in any case. She inquired whether he needed the rope for more than an hour. He calculated. She waited.

It depends, he finally answered.

On what?

On Last Minute Qualms, he said quickly.

She nodded. Someone had definitely called someone's bluff, but Maurice was not sure who'd called whose.

But surely, she said, those only last a minute?

A misnomer, obviously.

Or else a very long minute, she replied. Hold on, I'll get the rope.

No, no, you first.

What a gentleman.

I mean, I can wait, if you are only going to be a short while, he said, now genuinely alarmed but about what he couldn't say.

Were you going to leave a note?

Maurice hesitated: he did not like to admit to writing anything. No, he said, or maybe; he hadn't thought that far. And you?

Oh no, she nearly smiled. I never do.

And she softly closed the door.

By this time Maurice had a full frown. Today he was supposed to have the last word, whatever that meant, and here he was after his preparations, shoes, teeth, curtains, perhaps a letter, a letter to state something to someone, what to whom, everything out the window now. He continued to frown. Minutes were being killed, massacred, between him and the closed door. He had not heard the sound of the lock this time, and he was washed with green dismay to think he had been miscast in the drama he had sought to direct.

Or else a very long minute, she had said and, he thought now, dared him.

By the time he opened the door, he had composed an argument. Having neighbours means living, he would say, it seemed inevitable and for that, in this time of interruptions, also good. He would say it, say it now – he would have said it if she had been there, but the room was empty, no rope dangling, not even a note in evidence.

Peripherally spotting the open window, he raced to it and saw first the knot, the knot superior to his own for being more elegant and less bulky. The rope was artfully tied to the fire escape's rusted frame, but where custom dictates that ropes should lower a dangling mass from the point of its anchoring, this rope committed an astounding *faux pas* of physics. Maurice almost unwillingly craned his neck upward to see the rope's loose end reaching for the sky and, at the farthest point in his vision, the importunate young woman steadily climbing into the clouds.

Absurd! said Maurice, relieved.

Constellation

On Friday night last, a meteorite careened through the earth's upper atmosphere and decimated, with as much precision as unholy speed, a convention hall at the southern outskirts of Rome. At the time the hall held some two hundred or more astrologers from around the world, who were starting what promised to be a successful conference with a reception that boasted twelve new wines vinted for the occasion by a Pisces who admitted that the merlot of his own sign was probably the best. The Disaster Team arrived promptly on the scene and registered official amazement, which was not muted in their highly technical but inconclusive report submitted a few weeks later: (1) that not a single conference participant could be found, alive or otherwise, amid the choking layers of smoke and ash; (2) that nothing else, not even the closest of the structures proximate to the hall, was damaged in any significant way; and (3) that the Romans were much more excited about the feats of the national team's goalie, a brash young man who promised that the next year's World Cup was already his.

Antonio "Zigzag" Zambini professed a story of an unlikely upbringing. His mother told him she had slept with over two hundred Italian men and saved a tiny sample of sperm from each, which on the day of his conception she had carefully mixed together and inserted in the correct place. The sports star was thus a son of the nation, prone to boasting about the strength and will of which he was the embodiment. A wily man who never passed up a chance to make a profit,

Zambini's stepfather took bets on the young boy's races against not only other, older and better trained youths, but even dogs and in a couple of instances a rabbit. On one occasion, when the dead heat of a midsummer Sicilian afternoon could not prohibit the business of racing, the stepfather was distracted an hour before the starting command by his competitors, whose lackeys meanwhile quietly attacked Zambini. Ten strong kicks to the testicles later, Zambini still won the race but was told he would never have children. His mother assented to his joining a youth soccer league mostly because her attention was focussed on furious divorce proceedings, from which she extracted means to live in relaxed comfort the rest of her years. Her only regret, she told a journalist nearly twenty years later, was that she failed to get possession of her ex-husband's favourite painting, a nude, to which he claimed he had given his soul.

There was little that was not conventional about the picture. Scattered dishes of fruit and the requisite lapdog, all faithful eyes, were placed around the moon-faced woman with generous thighs. She did not look pleased to be painted. An expert would have recognized the usual influences, before pointing out that the thing was done certainly no later than 1890; it is less likely that, except for the scrawled signature beneath the edge of an olive carpet in the lower right corner, a name for the painter could have been produced. Eduardo Dana had been an inconspicuous man despite himself. He proposed to three women in the course of his lifetime, one of them twice, and the rejections had been in every case short and somewhat amazed. When he visited prostitutes, he found himself unable to initiate anything serious, so he began to draw and paint these compliant women who took his money and usually forgot about him. If they were properly studied, all of Dana's nudes would show a narrative in series: the faces grow younger while the sheets and decor around them age. None of the fruit in the pictures is eaten for, although a few bites can be seen to have been taken in the earlier works, no cores, seeds, stones, or pits are anywhere in evidence. An attentive Dana-watcher would notice that the dog is always the same dog, except in the last few pictures, where the madam has replaced the recently expired animal with a cat.

This cat loathed being in a bordello, and frequently tried to escape. Its most ingenious attempt involved crouching hidden within the open pack of a patron who, by his own admission, never stayed in any one place for long. Unfortunately, he also had an allergy to cats, and the prisoner was remanded to custody quickly enough. For weeks afterward the cat sulked, hardly comforted by the way the fattest of the heavenly bawds proffered her suffocating embraces without occasion. Just as hope was fading, one night the cat had a fantastic dream. In this dream, the cat was no longer a cat but instead a sailor, rather like one of the crew who had visited the bordello the previous summer.

Across his back were tattooed the names of his friends. Friendship meant everything to him, though in truth not more than the sea did, for in his heart the sea and friendship were one and the same. He could not swim: that was the trick of it. On almost every voyage some cursed thing, be it a high wind or a cannon's blow or the flailing of a kraken's tentacle, conspired to knock him into the drink, and in each case he had been rescued by someone whose name was then inscribed upon his sun-drenched body. Finally, one rescuer whose name had yet to be added to the record suggested he give the sailor the power to swim in a magic ritual. The sailor agreed and was told to eat nothing but fish until he observed a gull with a certain marking perch upon the ship. When this bird, blinking as if impatient, did appear, the sailor obeyed the strange instructions of the magician and told the bird that he wanted to dive without fear, to float without effort, to propel without fatigue. With a strange knife provided by the magician, the sailor cut off his smallest toe and handed it to the gull, who swallowed it greedily. The gull advised the sailor that, on his next birth-day, he would swim like an eel. However, if he fell into any deep waters before that day, he would sink heavier than the ship's anchor. In a fit of vexation the sailor killed the bird, and within moments a mighty storm blew up overhead, which eventually capsized the ship.

Count Tomasso Alessandro Lustro was less than pleased to hear that his cargo was lost to Neptune's depths. Although his fortune was unassailably vast, he was a devoted collector of oddities, and took great pride in his unmatched galleries of shrunken heads, shells, occult manuscripts, poisons, drums and stringed instruments, barbarian helmets, large birds, vol-canic ash samples, and magnifying glasses. Both his anger and his joy were received in extremes by his retinue of catamites, adolescents who together spoke more languages than they had thumbs. Their thrashings for the month following the loss of Lustro's consignment of Hindu statues became more than the local populace, typically more or less inured to their extrava-gant nobleman's peccadilloes, could countenance. By torch-light they ransacked his palace, unhalted by the guards, the night the cries of one young man were silenced by death. Lustro was judged by an *ad hoc* jury and told to choose between public castration and lifetime exile. Rather than leave his treasures, damaged though they were by the riot, Lustro elected the former punishment.

Having read of this incident, a woman in San Francisco con-vinced her fellow band members that a song about it ought to be included on their first album, which badly needed a closing number. She argued that here was a perfectly good allegory about capitalism, and when the drummer, who was recognized by all to be the least talented member of the group, asked what it meant, she scowled at her and said it didn't matter. "Cut off" did not win airtime anywhere in the United States, although several other songs on the album, such as "Stardust Tickles" and "Does It Hang Together?" became popular favourites in some college radio stations. It was a different story in Buenos Aires, however. "Cut off" there became a rallying cry among young girls not yet eligible to vote, and the album was cited for years afterwards as a source of creative inspiration for poets, photographers, historians, philosophers, and legal experts.

One explanation for this phenomenon came from a Welsh professor of linguistics. In a long series of letters to the British newspapers, the professor propounded a complicated theory about the sonic deflections of this particular recording and their interactions with sunspot emissions. Much of this argument, newspaper editors quickly saw, was incoherent, but that fact has never in itself prevented publication, and readers seemed to find the professor a great deal more entertaining than either the headlines or the so-called funny pages. In his last letter – allegedly written just before he thickly lined his study with cork and locked himself inside, never to emerge again – the professor noted that even the repercussions of the press dotting his last period in the last edition to run that letter could set off a chain of events so curious and terrible as to defy understanding. This farce, insofar as it was not too late or simply impossible to do otherwise, he, the undersigned professor emeritus, would not be party to, and he advised everyone in good conscience to shut up immediately.

When she read this, Inge let out a hiccup, a tic which used to be defensive but since her husband had died had become instead the register of her contempt. Now that her husband was gone her hatred had no specific target, and in honest moments she reflected that even she was taken aback at how much she reviled everything and everyone around her. The newspaper in her hands, for example, was really substandard, full of lies and spelling errors, and even the ink quality was laughable. Those whose tragedies made the front page were idiots who deserved worse than they'd got, and those who wrote the tragedies were opportunist scum, lucky to have jobs at all. And here, turning to the horoscopes, she found idiocy, mendacity, a gigantic waste of time. A survivor of several wars and more men, Inge was riding the crest of a very high wave, a veritable tsunami of enmity at the moment when she read her own horoscope and, overcome by its atrociousness, toppled forward from her wheelchair.

The doctor takes her pulse but is thinking about a movie whose name he cannot remember, if he ever knew it. He has been having an awful week and two nights ago to clear his head he wandered alone into a cinema, as he has not done in years. In the movie a man had been running through a desert, for some reason, and there was a woman, or two women, expecting him to call. He might have been from another planet. There had been some trouble, a conflict between himself and someone in an office, perhaps one of the women. There was a fan overhead in the office and it played tricks on the shadows along the wall. It had not seemed like an interesting film but there it is, worrying his mind all that much later. The doctor records the time of death and trudges to the next case.

The Tip

for Dean J. Irvine

I was not a poet. The confirmation was exact, and timed with the arrival of our disinterested server, a thin girl with a fat pouting bottom lip, with our fourths on a tray. We were very much ensconced in a booth decorated with photos of dead jazz musicians, both of us pink-faced and for the moment silent, but each for his own reasons. Aspern offered to the girl his slightest smile as he took the pints in hand, but as I had already noticed with no warmth, she did not know a poet from a fencepost. Although Aspern conveyed no sense of any slight, I was indignant for the both of us.

No clean route of return was left to the conversation: after the bombshell, only a crater to circumnavigate. I toyed with my drink – meaning my hands were never away from it, as opposed to the sheaf of papers and notebook likewise clutched before then, and I took large, regular gulps – while Aspern spoke in a voice not unkind about the inadequacy of the idea of *vocation*. He declared *vocation* a mystic's archaic and emptyheaded word. Infrequent but very uncustomary uses of hard expletives suggested that by now even he felt the effects of the drink.

Although it may be to no purpose, and I probably lack the ability to express it with any justice, it ought to be recorded that Aspern drank like a poet. I don't mean anything grotesque, such as that he slurped back gross quantities; though certainly he could hold his own. Style! On previous occasions, usually when there were more than just the two of us around just such a table, I could quietly and unreservedly admire the manner in which he held his glass, or even how he set it down. The shaping of his lips to the rim had a delicacy and also a sly hint of the insincere which the most gorgeous movie stars and figures in paintings could not match with their whispers and kisses.

Vocation! His mouth screwed up. Emptyheaded word. As bad, nearly, as *talent* or *inspiration* – though at least those things exist, after a fashion, but not in the fashion of those words. Cash and breath, that's what they mean. Indispensables. Shoot for those.

Let me make my point, he said, with a story.

There must be any number of wrong ways in which to tell this pathetic little story, and this is only one of them. Most of it is true, and some of it is relevant, which all in all is not a bad mixture.

I know of a poet, or I used to know about one, living near my miserable little hometown which barely kissed the main roads between cities before it prissily moved back into rustic obscurity. This man, this poet I'm talking about, had a large and remote house in which, rumours said, he lived all by his lonesome. Not that he was never seen. He was one of those old bachelors who like to take long country walks, and the two unmarried librarians in the town, sisters who poured scorn on anybody who dared even to bother them at their paper-shuffling posts, competed for his attention during his regular visits there. It wasn't that he was handsome, or even an exceptionally snappy dresser. Those jaded sisters smelled *culture* on him, something they'd not sniffed since getting stuck in this backwoods, and the first time he came in to the library and gently asked, please, did they happen to have a copy of *Fêtes galantes* he could borrow – well, that was that – *nous aimions ce jeu de dupes*. Apparently, he read just about everything, and the idea that he might be rich surely was no impediment to romantic fancies.

Might be rich, I said. Obviously he was a man of means, if that phrase still has any clean use in it, for the fact of that huge place of his. And then there was the semi-mystery of his professional past, as it became known he was once a physician who had fairly recently given up his practice. He was not old enough to have retired, but there was no perceptible cloud of shame hovering anywhere about him: it must have been the effect of a weariness, or detected unsuitability, within himself, that explained the surrender. For a while local people liked to speculate on the question.

The giddy librarians were among the most indulgent in this diversion, egging each other on probably both for sheer delirium and in secret hopes of observing the other slip in her necessary balance between devotion and decorum. Gradually the competition grew fiercer, until the day of the younger sister's coup: the discovery (after the unmentioned fact of several weeks of private research) of a slim, green-covered volume of poems authored by none other than the gentleman doctor. By the time of her modest announcement of this happy accident, she had, she blushed to demonstrate to the small crowd of the Friends of the Library gathered around her, found some idle moments in which to memorize some of the verses.

Of course, the morning after the unusually celebratory evening's meeting, a garotte of cool silence was tightening around the library. The two sisters had little to say to one another, and the due dates stamped by the elder sister in books borrowed that day were more indelible than ever before. The nose out of joint abruptly straightened with a vengeance one autumn day when there came the supremely casual counter-announcement: the Friends were all invited to a *soirée de poésie* later that month which the good doctor would attend (sensation) and perhaps might be convinced to give a reading (greater sensation). Apparently the elder sister had been in postal communication with the gentleman. One septuagenarian Friend gave an encouraging leer and wink, smooth work my dear, which action released unexpected acids into the younger sister's digestive system. She sought release that evening, shut in her room in their shared house, with a bottle of red wine she'd been saving for a happier occasion. It was, if not the absolute beginning, the decisive turn of a fatal alcoholism.

Energies sprang up in both sisters to focus on the approaching date of the *soirée*. Neither of them could speak to a person without mentioning it – oh, perhaps some cheese and wine with grapes, nothing too extravagant, but all the same quite marvellous, I don't mind telling you we're very excited – and at least the sleep of the elder librarian was sometimes troubled by the thought of a last-minute cancellation from the guest of honour.

There were some grounds for worry. What the doctor had accepted was a vague invitation to a literary evening, nothing that explicitly called for any contribution of performance on his part. And, finally, on the evening of the *soirée* (black rain, I remember, straight down most of the night), the first thing the librarians noticed of the doctor's shyly punctual appearance was the lack of a briefcase, folder, satchel, or anything which might carry verses. One sister gave a searching look to the other, who pretended not to notice. There was still the green-covered volume on hand should the need (more need than occasion here) arise. And the wine was opened.

Almost immediately the doctor began to feel uncomfortable, pawed as he was by cooing Friends, each of whom seemed to use strange and stranger innuendo when speaking to him. Yes, he admitted, he did enjoy poetry, and when he admitted it another would more than enjoy poetry right back; when he uttered the name of a poet, with a profession of admiration, the name was echoed back to him couched in deeper and inevitably longer professions of feeling surpassing admiration. But at the same time there was always a gesture of deference to his authority. One or another librarian reached over to fill his glass and exchange a smile. Nothing he said went unattended, or indeed without some fairly enthusiastic reaction. Warmth spread through his little ears: the wine was creeping up on him fast, he was not used to it. Then there was a hand on his shoulder, rather near the neck. It was the younger librarian, herself not untouched by the wine, asking him directly whether he felt ready to offer some of his work. The hand remained on his shoulder.

His work? He flushed and shook. He looked around him at the eager stares. His work? No, no. Impossible, he was shaking his head and putting down his glass on the most immediate surface. The citric smell of the younger librarian's perfume crept into his nostrils as she was naming the title of his little collection; he then shook his head even more violently, and moved to where his coat was hanging. No, he stammered only part of an explanation, those words dissatisfied him more than they could know; he was sorry; he was not prepared; he was very sorry. And then he was out the door. It was still fairly early, one of the Friends observed sourly.

Miserable, the retired doctor walked through the night and rain without the umbrella he had forgotten at the library but which he correctly assumed he would never recover. (I once heard that, years later, the elder librarian kept it as a cherished object, and in her lonely senior years never went out in any weather without it.) His lips were this moment drawn tight, the next quivering with half-words muttered to himself. By the time (over an hour and a half later) he reached his door and tremblingly pushed and turned the key, his approbations were nearly audible. What a fool!

Once inside he strode directly to the bathroom and dried his head with a towel. What a fool! Again and again. He could still smell the librarian's perfume. The mirror dutifully showed his vanity's incongruence with his pitiful drenched appearance. Briskly switching off the light, he stepped into the hallway and towards the staircase. He halted at its base and slowly stooped to see the carpet soiled there by a muddy boot's imprint.

All of his thoughts were rerouted by this discovery. No sound. His eyes flashed in the hall as he thought of the pistol he kept in his office, which was not far. Still no sound. He crept like a man unaccustomed to creeping to the office, and stepped inside its darkness, reaching for the lamp.

It sparked alive before he could reach it.

Our fifths. Aspern grinned at me as he gestured for me to hurry up with my unfinished glass. That from him was pretty much all I completely understood at this point. Actually, I experienced an unknown tinge of resentment: though slight, it was altogether new. He quaffed the better part of his drink before he continued:

Which he apprehended first the doctor probably would not have been able to tell: the presence of the stranger comfortable in the chair holding that sought-after pistol, or the disarray that surrounded the two men. As for the first, a closer inspection revealed a much younger man than himself, an insouciant face, but one with telltale signs of surprise that belied his show of armed and seated ease. The mess of the room, meanwhile, was certainly the effect of a thorough ransacking.

The doctor was ordered, with an accompanying wave of the pistol probably learned from gangster films, to sit down, on the floor. For some reason the burglar, when he began to speak, often addressed the other man as "sir," though without irony. But he was straight to the point: Where did the gentleman store his money? Was there a safe in the house? No, the doctor admitted, ashamed by the vulgarity of discussing money, no safe. What hiding place, then? (For it was clear the thief had been in the house for some time, searching, opening, loosing, breaking, without any other result than frustration.)

No hiding place, beyond the drawers already lying upturned on the floor – which the thief promptly seized and scanned for false bottoms, whereupon the doctor told him they had none. The amount found in those drawers ("sir") was negligible. The thief wasn't to be taken for a fool. A man of the doctor's class and esteem had to have more valuables: what about jewellery, trinkets, collectibles? He waved the gun again, but it was even more clear then that he had never held such a thing before. The doctor watched the tremors of the wrist, and wondered about this youth: he was not from the town, but very likely from a neighbouring area. After a moment he answered that he had no collateral that would interest the thief. All that he had was the house; he was not a rich man.

Sitting further back in the chair, the thief scratched his head and exhaled slowly. He took his eyes from the doctor for the first time and silently looked around him a moment. Not a rich man, he repeated, and pointed the pistol at a much-dented metal box sitting in a far corner of the room, asking, then what do you keep such a thing like that for? It had taken forever to open! And what was in it? Papers – not stocks or credit notices or anything – just scribblings! With this growl the thief bounded over to the box and lifted out a sheaf of papers. Why should they be locked up in such a box, hidden beneath other papers in a cabinet? Throwing the papers down before the doctor: were these valuable?

These, the doctor admitted, were poems. He was very private about his literary work, and did not like to show it to anyone until he was certain – well, he finished lamely.

The thief sat down again. Poems, he reflected. He had known, of course, about the *soirée* at the library, widely spoken about; how the gentleman was almost certainly going to give a reading of good duration; how he was a poet; though it was the fact of a rich man's absence from his house that had primarily held the thief's attention. Sure, he had had some acquaintance with literature, back in school; some of it was all right. Poems, he said, looking down at the floor. Lots of them, judging from the quantity of pages.

Unexpected by either of them, especially the doctor, came the note of pride in his answer: A life's work. He had hopes of recognition as a major poet. When? Well, the doctor hesitated, and the thief interrupted by asking to hear a poem. Strangely the unpleasant forces crushing him at the library seemed so much more awful than this, to have a stranger with a weapon before him. A command performance, if you will. The doctor smiled.

He read a poem, and then another, and then ("go on, sir") another, without once picking himself up from the floor or, indeed, growing any less pleased about the bizarre circumstances which allowed him to redeem his evening's poor showing. After a dozen verses, the thief set down the pistol beside him, and after three or four more he barked with approval at the wit, at the grace of them. One of them reminded him of his mother's death, of the ever-freshness of that wound; another articulated his own curiosity about the meaning of dreams. Together they flashed excited glances, and like conspirators finally huddled together on the floor surrounded by the pages, a newly opened bottle of wine between them. Their hearts glowed. Those were almost definitely the happiest hours of the good doctor's life.

Aspern finished his drink, and admitted that he had to go. Any more, he said, and he'd need a wheelbarrow and a stronger fellow than me to drive it. He gave a rude laugh and tapped my notebook as he stood up and stretched. I looked down to see there the bill and, confused with more than drink, pulled out my wallet. Aspern was already lumbering towards the door, and I caught up with him before we had to part ways on the street, to breathe a half-question:

And the doctor – ?

If Aspern heard me, he did not reply, as he ambled down the street and stopped on the corner before turning out of sight, whereupon he pointed his forefinger and cocked his thumb at me with a grin. The feeling of my hand against the door barely registered as I held it standing there at the threshold, watching him go, and my first intake of night air went unappreciated. Over my shoulder I caught sight of the lightly waving hand of our server, who had probably just discovered the generous tip I had left.

Way to Go

My mind is made up. *An interesting phrase*. I have made up my mind. I am leaving. Before I leave, though, I thought you might like to know why. *Why what?* I thought you might like to know why I've decided to leave. Why I'm leaving. After all this time. And right after I've explained why, I am going to open that door and leave. I am going to march over to that door, throw it open, and leave, and that will be the end. *The end of what?* I knew you would ask that, I just knew it. For a long time I thought the problem was communication, that there was no communication, no dialogue. Then I realized, though not until a long time after that, that there was plenty of communication, lots of dialogue, nothing but communication and dialogue. Like I said, it took me a long time to appreciate that. So then I supposed that the problem was understanding. There was so much dialogue, so much unremitting communication, but no understanding. Jabbering on, that's all there was, meaningless intercourse. *An interesting phrase*. Meaningless discourse. I once knew a guy who had a budgerigar, and as I thought about this problem of mine, I remembered how he complained he couldn't sleep for the prattling on of this bird. It seems this budgerigar had in his tenure at the pet store collected a cranium's fill of inanities and so all day and all night the thing cooed and squawked about how good and hungry and lovely and handsome and clever it was. Finally the guy gave the bird a mirror. For the first few hours it was business as usual, though the bird was addressing all of its usual self-congratulatory remarks to its reflection. Then the cage fell silent. Its owner fell asleep easily that night but died of a massive stroke in the early hours. When I thought of this incident I reflected, oh, but don't say that's an interesting phrase. *How is it interesting?* Hardly at all, it wasn't even worth bringing it up, but it does illustrate my old theory about sleep not being worth the effort. Really, I hate sleep. And it's not because I have bad dreams, not that I want to get into that. Who was it, some poet or other, said there's nothing so boring as other people's dreams? Well, my dreams are like that: listening to other people's dreams. It's like dreaming secondhand, as though my dreams have already been enjoyed by somebody else, somebody they were prepared for, not me. That's why I hate sleep, that and it's so undignified. That's also one of the reasons I am leaving. All I do here is sleep. This place inspires nothing else. The ceiling beckons to be snored at. Now that I think about it, there's a colourlessness about this place, as though the walls won't commit to an honest hue. Soporific by design. I get weary just talking about it. *Would you like to sleep now?* Some days it almost resembles a sense of humour, your need to know every pointless little thing. Of course I don't want to sleep now, that's what I'm saying, a problem of communication, that's certain. I once knew a guy who told his wife about a dream he'd had the night before, and this dream comes to my mind now because it was about how he was leaving her, his wife, but was taking a long time about it. He had this huge suitcase into which he was placing all of his things, and though the case swallowed them whole as though they were drops of rain falling into an ocean, so that the space in the case was infinite, he could not finish packing and even found himself worrying about whether the case could hold all of his possessions, which seemed endless. It was a maddening situation, he told his wife. She burst into tears and fled the room. It seems this guy's wife figured that his dream meant he was trying to leave her, and this interpretation left her inconsolable. For the rest of the day her husband cajoled, reasoned, comforted, wheedled, but to no avail. When at last he gave up, he laid down on the sofa and had a fatal aneurism. Sometimes when I'm about to go to sleep I think about that. Not when I'm really exhausted, you know, I mean when I'm tossing and turning. *An interesting phrase.* A corny one, you mean. I doubt anybody really tosses and turns. It's mostly a matter of lying there, of being horizontal and thinking about the very fact of being horizontal. Tossing and turning sounds like an adventure in comparison. When I was just a squirt, my room's ceiling was stucco and in my sleepless imagination I sanded and smoothed away all of that awful rugosity, scraping my knuckles as I went. Actually I'm not sure I ever finished, I mean that I ever imagined completing this chore, which seemed to go on forever. Maybe the exhaustion involved even in thinking about that kind of work got me to sleep. I hated that room. This one reminds me of it, at least in as much as it provokes my loathing, too. Used to be, for a very short time, that there was a little satisfaction to be had in that, just loathing, looking at the ceiling and loathing as time went by. Now I loathe the loathing. I've stayed here for so long. *Why?* There's always a lower circle in hell. Tortoises all the way down. *Why tortoises?* You know,

the thing about a terrapin
is that he totes his house with him.

There's that story about some physicist or other who gets confronted after some lecture by the lady who tells him the universe is carried on the back of a tortoise, and it's tortoises all the way down. I guess I thought everybody knew that one. I once knew a guy who used to run every day. He had a severe sort of routine. He would start in the morning and run a long distance directly away from his starting point. Only when he was absolutely breathless with exhaustion, when his knees quivered and his soles burned, did he stop, and then, then he would turn around and run back as best he could, often as not limping, clutching at posts and handholds, chewing his tongue in pain. He used to say he was the hare in flight and the tortoise in return, that's what makes me think of him. As this routine wore on, he was running further and further from home and returning later and later in the day. He used to say that eventually he would never have to stop running, would never have to return, unless he ran so far and so long that he wound up again where he started. Before that happened, though, both of his lungs burst apart one morning at breakfast, even before he'd started the day's mad run. Which just goes to prove what I've been saying, if you're going to go, go all the way. *All the way where?* Away from here, away from this. Away. *Whither?* Oh come on, nobody uses words like that anymore. That's part of the problem, this is all so old, so done. I need something new, something rejuvenating. *What?* Well, I don't know, but I won't find it here. *Why not?* I've been trying to explain that, all this time that's what I've been trying to do. I should have known it was useless. *Why?* Why what? *Why?* That's it, it's over, I'm leaving, I'm going. You hear, that's it, I'm going. All these useless questions, all these useless explanations. This is it, this is the end. *The end of what?* Please, just, please stop. *Stop what?* Don't. See, I'm going. Don't. *Don't what?* Don't ask.

Good Faith

Mighty proud I am that I am able to have a spare bed for my friends.

– Samuel Pepys

That reminds me of a story of which in retrospect you think, now that was pretty funny, the way that happened. Not that it's such a big deal, you know, but there's something about it that's funny and those kinds of funny things make you think. And this is just an ordinary day as the background, so it's not as though there's anything special about that. We were just heading out for an evening drink, to get some fresh air – this is the usual people in this case: Grant and Yellow and myself – after one phone call prompted another, the way these connections start.

So out we go. And when you go out like this it usually happens you meet somebody else who'll go along with you all, and that's again pretty much just another natural connective link. We run into Scotty, whom we all haven't seen in a little while, and isn't it the funniest thing but he's got this talking dog. Grant asked Scotty where he found his companion, and Scotty said he too was just out for a little stroll, maybe to call on this girl he's been seeing, and this dog comes up to him on the street and talks to him.

What did it say? asked Grant.

Why don't you ask the dog? Scotty replied. You could tell he didn't want Grant to be rude like he could often be when he wasn't watching what he was saying.

It was nothing really, said the dog. It was nothing much more than chit-chat. I was just feeling a little talkative and there was nobody around 'til Scott shows up.

We call him Scotty, Yellow explained. It's never Scott. We always call him Scotty. I don't remember why exactly.

Names are funny things, the dog said philosophically, and we all nodded quietly. Take me for example. I can't tell you my name, as you tell me yours, because of course my name is something you smell, rather than hear.

That makes sense, Scotty said to us, because dogs rely on the sense of smell for most of their information.

So there's no real way for me to translate my name, said the dog, by way of apology in case we thought he was just being snobbish. Yellow made a joke about how he had drank before with people whose names he did not know and so one more instance certainly wouldn't be out of character. This seemed to set everybody much more at ease and so walking resumed.

I once drank for most of a night with a woman who turned out to be a man, Grant announced. It was a strange situation. There we were, both getting pretty close to pissdom and going on about wage freezes and good restaurants and whatever else and she gives me a stare and says very matter-of-factly, it might interest you to know that I'm not exactly a woman.

Yellow wanted to know what Grant had said to that.

Well, said Grant. I asked, how exactly? And she said, it's just a matter of a few inches.

It's hard to say who laughed hardest at that. Yellow almost walked into a post, while the dog and Scotty barked together. The dog admitted he loved a good joke, and in his time he had often strained to hear them. Grant then mentioned that I had a good memory for such things but I just smiled, because I didn't have anything to compete with his funny story.

We got to Hurley's just then, and settled ourselves as the waitress slowly made her way over to us. She had a pretty smile, and while you may say a lot of waitresses have pretty smiles, it's a matter of fact that only a few have sincere pretty smiles. Most of them aren't smiling at you sincerely. The waitress on this particular evening, I recall, had a sincere pretty smile. It's funny things like that you remember about a place, an evening.

No sooner had we ordered than who should come up to us but Eric. He had been there a little while, it seemed, and he said he was just on his way out when he happened to catch sight of us.

How long's it been since I saw you? Grant laughed.

You okay? asked Yellow. You look pretty tired.

I might sleep more if there weren't so many knocks at my bedroom door, Eric said, and everybody ooohed. The waitress returned with a pitcher and Grant paid for it.

Those young boys getting to be too much for you, Grant said, and he poured a glass for Eric, but Eric said he couldn't stay.

Actually, said Eric, I'm having trouble with the type that keeps on trying...you might think he would, though. Think he's gotten it before once or twice, from what I understand.

Who's the suitor? asked Grant, who drank the glass himself.

Travis, said Eric.

Travis is gay? I asked. I'd been silent awhile but this was pretty hard to believe.

And I thought he just couldn't get any girls, said Yellow.

I expect it's easier not to get them, said Scotty, when you're not exactly trying.

That set everybody laughing, especially Grant and the dog, who slapped each other's backs a couple of times before they settled and Eric repeated that it was a fact. It seems that Travis was making a habit of late night calls, and prolonged conversations with Eric at parties and so on.

I don't believe we've met, Eric said to the dog, and we made some quick introductions, during which the dog again courteously explained how his name suffered in translation.

Sure you can't stay for a glass? asked Grant.

Oh, positive, Eric laughed lightly. I wonder if he's ever stayed for a glass, I can't remember him ever doing so. There are certain people, you know, who always seem to be flying by and can never stay for a glass. I wish I could, really, he said, and I'm sorry to have to run.

You've got to quit apologizing, Yellow put in. Did you ever know someone who apologized so much as he does?

Sorry, I'll try, said Eric, who then blushed a little.

Oh never mind, Yellow said, and grinned at Scotty, who was busy looking a little over his shoulder at this girl talking to the bartender. There used to be a funny story at the time that Scotty had not seen any action since the last time the Queen visited, and because of it Scotty was teased about always waiting for royalty. Though it should be mentioned that the girl he was then looking at was worth the effort, and I myself missed seeing Eric dart out the door.

Well, within minutes of Eric passing through, Amanda shows up with some friend of hers. Nobody caught her name. Amanda has this mumbling problem sometimes, and other times she just talks too fast. She says they've just had the same idea of going out for a drink. She tells me on the side when they've sat down how her friend, whatever her name was, needs some cheering up because her boyfriend is travelling in Europe and she thinks he's cheating on her there. I think I just nodded. What are you supposed to say?

Amanda offered to buy the next pitcher, and that made Grant warm up to her. He never really cared for her much. The dog tried striking up a conversation with Amanda's friend but she just had this blank look most of the time and though I couldn't hear what exactly they were talking about, I can well imagine it wasn't really very engrossing.

How are you doing, anyway? Amanda asked me.

[The thing is that I've always been what my friends would call a private sort of person. The people who really know me would call me that. Emotions tend to stay inside, and work themselves out that way. Better that way, pride tells me. Better that way than to dump a lot of unnecessary stuff on somebody who probably has worse things to bear. It's funny the way you deal with problems, the way you weigh them and judge them. Some bad things strike some people as really awful, but you can always find somebody else who has worse troubles, or who thinks that thing that's got you down is really a good thing. When I think about these things, because you've got to think about them, I know that's why I play my cards so close to the chest. Life's a funny thing. You never know what people will think, so who's to say what they might feel?]

Not too bad, I tell Amanda when she asks how I'm doing.

Why don't you ask me? Scotty said.

I know exactly how you are, Amanda told him. She turned to the dog, who had just given up trying to talk to whatever-her-name-was. What do you do? she asked.

I'm unemployed at the moment, said the dog. Grant poured him another glass when he said that.

Oh let's not talk about unemployment, jobs, job interviews, or any of that, Scotty said quickly. No, we're not going to talk about that stuff tonight if I have anything to do with it.

Well, Amanda smiled and said. What would you really like to talk about?

Scotty rubbed his chin and slowly said: Why don't we talk about something a little deeper. More philosophical.

The existence of God in fifty words or less, Grant laughed. Prove or disprove conclusively. Questions from the floor afterwards.

No, it's a good idea, the dog nodded at Scotty.

I don't want to talk about God, Amanda said and crossed her arms. I had to put up with enough God in my childhood.

The devil then, Scotty said to her, and dramatically winked. Maybe you need the devil for your adult years.

We could all use more of the devil, Grant put in.

The devil is fine with me, said Amanda, as a subject for Scotty's deep philosophical conversation.

I met the devil once, Yellow said, and everyone looked at him because he sounded serious for the first time that night.

Did you vote for him? asked the dog, laughing.

I'm not talking, Yellow started, and had trouble working out the word "figuratively." I really met the devil. It was one night, late I seem to remember but in any event it was fairly dark and cool. This is some years ago.

What did he do? Amanda asked.

He came up to me and asked if I wanted my dreams to come true, Yellow said in a low voice. No warm-up, just out of the blue like that. Pretty bold, don't you think?

The devil's not supposed to be modest, I said.

What'd you do? Scotty asked him.

I told him I wasn't interested, Yellow said, and drank proudly.

How'd you know he was the devil? asked Scotty.

Yellow gave him a stern look for asking such a thing. He said: He was evil, obviously.

He was evil? Scotty wondered.

Evil itself, Yellow said with conviction.

Before solemn silence could start, the waitress reappeared, and Yellow told her we could do with another.

Can I ask you a professional question? Grant said to her before she moved away. She nodded. He went on: Our friend here was just telling us about how he once met the devil, and I have doubts about the matter myself. Maybe you can clear this up for us. Have you ever seen the devil, by any chance?

The waitress laughed. Oh, I think he's been in here for a drink a couple of times.

Yellow frowned a little at Grant, who replied, How would you describe him, then? I mean, how did you know he was the devil?

The waitress moved her weight to her other leg and considered. I'm not sure, exactly, she said finally. I suppose it was the horns.

Again Grant and the dog collided together with laughter, and Amanda giggled along with them, probably because they looked so funny together.

Amanda's friend said at this point she had to get going. Grant and the dog didn't really notice as they were still kind of sniggering. Watch you don't run into the devil on your way out, Grant managed to say, but she might not have heard. Amanda smiled and went behind her friend.

You know something? Scotty said after they went. Amanda is looking really good these days.

Did anybody catch her friend's name? Yellow asked, grinning. I think he had decided not to be the serious one anymore. Everybody just grinned, said this or that about how they just missed it.

We drank a lot more that night, and talked more, too, and we soon went our separate ways. That isn't what makes this thing so funny, though, because what I'm getting to concerns the other day, maybe a few days after that.

I was out again, I don't remember where I was going at the time. Suddenly this woman comes up to me, asking, hey, how are you? And it takes me a long moment before I realize that it's Amanda's friend from that night! She remembered exactly who I was, and was really friendly this time, saying how she had been in a bit of a funk that night, and I said we all have those times, or something like that. Then she asked me, after we talked a little bit longer, if I wanted to go out again some time and she laughed that she would try to be a bit more sociable this time. And I said that sounded okay.

Which just goes to show you, I guess, how funny it is the way people get along. It's just the weird things like that, you only think of them afterwards, and then it's a little hard to believe it all happened like that at the time.

Solacium

Dear Ms. Heath,

His Holiness, most disturbed by your recent letter, has seen fit to appoint me to reply to it, inasmuch as I am able. Before I set about doing so directly, however, there are one or two points which I feel ought to be expressed so as to avoid any misunderstandings.

First of all, I regret to report that His Holiness is in a very poor state of health presently, and though you should not worry yourself that your comments, however upsetting to His Holiness, have caused or contributed to his decline, you must understand that these are the very real extenuating circumstances which prevent him from replying to you personally, as I feel confident he would otherwise certainly do.

The second point, again made in anticipation of a query you might reasonably have in mind, if not upon your lips at this very moment, concerns the authority with which I write. If not His Holiness, you may well wonder, then who is it that can assume to speak in reply? And upon glancing at the signature below, you may feel disappointed to see not the mark of a bishop, or of any more eminently respectable position than that of a novice; and as a result, you may prematurely feel your words have not been treated at all properly.

I assure you this is not so. Novice though I may be, my devotion to the Church and to His Holiness (may God bring him health) is such that it defies my clumsy framework of language. (Writing to you in English, I must tell you, is an additional pleasure in the exercise, as I have been very busy studying it of late and to be honest, Latin can wear thin after a while.) In fact, I found your appeal to His Holiness so earnest, so worthy of genuine consideration and response, despite the occasion of this unforeseen ill health of His Holiness, that I must tell you I personally sought out your letter from the considerably heavy files of correspondence housed here and campaigned (if that is not too strong a word) for its relevance until a reply was recently deemed "necessary" (exact word). You might say I took up the assignment.

I hope this makes clear my position, as well as the position of His Holiness, and the context of this writing.

Now, to your letter:

I will not insult your intelligence – to which quality the style of your letter eminently testifies – by reciting to you the importance of the vow of celibacy, which vow the members of my calling, including His Holiness in particular, believe in fitfully (right word?). However, in light of this vow and its importance, the characteristics you attribute to His Holiness in your letter, while arguably perceptive (there has been some agreement by a minority of the ordained who have encountered your letter, though of course this is simply idle talk and not a Church statement), are inapplicable.

Your devotion to His Holiness is both unquestionable and effusive, and the staying power and sincerity of your words are what have continually struck me as I have re-read your letter these past few evenings. However, I feel compelled to note the difference between "devotion" and "attraction." Though these are both fine Latinate words, the first has a greater Christian resonance in its relation to giving, as a promise is given, than the latter word, whose etymology betrays a basis in taking. The truest Christian passion exists within a state of selflessness.

Also, earthly forms of Christian love at their most powerful supercede the narrow focus a momentary desire likely necessarily creates. Your letter's reference to the matter of His

Holiness being "the only man" capable of the miracles you ably describe is certainly evidence of this bias (though these acts are not, His Holiness would very likely have you know, miracles as they are recognized by the Church). When you implore His Holiness to recognize your "needs" (and I was relieved and pleased to see you sign yourself "Ms."), you do not recognize that the earthly needs of a good Christian never depend upon another Christian's neglect of his unearthly (which is to say, holy and spiritual) affairs.

Then, Ms. Heath, there is the matter of your "prayers," which in my capacity of (de facto) spokesperson for His Holiness I am afraid I cannot choose to overlook. "Praying" to God in Heaven to have His Holiness perform with you (or for that matter with anyone else) the acts you have, as you put it yourself, "so long dreamt of, thought about, longed for" is not, it has been agreed upon here, a proper prayer for a loving Christian. I myself am not a member of the many who hold that, indeed, your confession is one of blasphemy; but I think this is because I am younger than many of my colleagues, and, if I may put it so, more of a man of the world. You may believe me when I say that I have spent a great deal of time and study turning over the problems mortal passion plays in the realm of the immortal soul.

While I admit some of your articulations, probably because they are in the North American idiom, are not entirely clear to me (for instance, I do not recognize the meaning in "I know you would reject the rubber, like a real man"), your trouble is evident enough. In good Christian faith you need to acknowledge what earthly hopes are viable in keeping a good relationship with God. At the same time, you might broaden the subject of your lively and very interesting passion, perhaps slowly at first, finding room in your heart not only for His Holiness (God restore him), ailing and eminently unavailable as he is, but for those around him, and the members of the Church, no matter how menial.

In this effort, please feel entirely free to seek from this quarter any instruction and support I can willingly give.

Romans 1:11-12

The Watch

He was a doorman and his friend was a doorman. There they were talking and he was saying yes we do have an unexamined role in society, I've put a lot of thought into that.

Not like we're invisible, his friend rejoined, though the way some of them walk by you'd be forgiven for thinking otherwise. Here the schism of debate opened. He disagreed with his friend in principle if not in fact for, to his mind, the watchword of the doorman is faith.

In what?

In the virtue, if you like, of those for whom we hold open the door, he said, and his voice's timbre showed a growing warmth to the subject. Holding further he said we have an eye, a critical eye, in our profession and we use it.

Scratching his beard, his friend admitted that there was something in that, of course he did not always open the door, he had certain responsibilities to the integrity of the establishment as did any doorman. The affirmative reply added that one often offered a form of salute while holding the door.

His friend cut in to say often, you mean always, least I always do, it's that sort of thing, that attention that makes a great doorman. He nodded at his friend and asserted it's faith that underwrites that attention you see.

No, I don't see.

I'll try to explain, let's go back to not opening the door.

Yes.

Why would you not open the door all the time if it's your job as a doorman?

His friend blinked and began to say confusedly well there are guests of the establishment and then there, oh ho, and his face assumed a slight leer, you're driving at the ethical conduct of the doorman.

Ethos has much to do with it, I suppose, said he, but you were going to say there are those who aren't guests and you don't hold the door open for them.

Unless they're guests' visitors, his friend put in.

He replied then you have to judge, discriminate, evaluate, and that takes the critical eye.

You say you've put a lot of thought into this but so far I don't see much evidence of anything beyond a rather uncomplicated exegesis of black and white regulations. This was said with a genial tone, for they had long been friends and doormen.

In my opinion, he answered in an equally genial tone, all serious acts of criticism stem from some faith, though perhaps the nature of that faith is unstated, in transition or even being criticized itself.

No need to get too heady all at once, I was just saying, but go on.

We are agreed, we have long been agreed, he said, that ours is without putting too fine a point on it a noble profession.

More than most understand, came the customary reply.

This nobility is part of a transference from the *a priori* nobility, arguably lesser or greater, of those for whom we hold open the door, in fact that crossing of the threshold, synchronized with the offering of a form of salute, could be considered the point or moment of that transference.

I take back what I said, chuckled his friend, you have definitely put thought into this, and I like to think I've followed you this far but you'll have to explain your thetic emphasis on faith.

He said well suppose in the course of your shift, and his friend interrupted with watch. The schism opened further while he and his friend realized they had a terminological divide between them, never before recognized, concerning the duty hours of the doorman. Eventually he deferred to his friend's use of the word watch, though not without commenting on its strangeness and prompting from his friend a digression from the dialogue in the form of an anecdotal defence of the usage of watch. I call it a watch, said his friend, more or less on account of the voyeuristic qualities encouraged and developed by years in the profession and my own appreciation of those qualities' primacy. Have I told you, his friend slowly asked him, of the night I left the door?

He looked at his friend with amazement and said no, you left the door, I can imagine anyone else but.

I left the door one night, his friend said. There was a lady who arrived at the door this night overburdened with packages, to this day I wonder what could have been in them to make them as heavy as they were and yet as fragile as she assured me they also were when I offered to help her, this was some time ago and one of those occasions when some seasonal virus had thinned the working personnel to a skeletal affair and left me with extra duties, and I did not know this woman but she was entirely a lady and had visible among the many objects she was juggling a set of keys, so I assisted with the heavy packages and found myself in the elevator with her for the elevator operator was among those recently dispatched by the virus and I listened to her apologize and though naturally I told her it was nothing, part of the job, a pleasure, and made other such pleasantries, it was becoming distressingly clear to me that she was somehow enjoying my discomfort, watching me repeatedly volleying harmless, charitable responses under the weight of the heavy packages.

What do you mean she enjoyed it?

His friend shrugged and scratched his beard again, this time more vigorously, and said and that's not all, she was looking at me and then not looking at me, I mean this lady was not unattractive but there was something in her eyelashes and it was very distracting because I couldn't determine what it was, not without openly staring at her and it was all I could do not to, but it goes back to what you were saying about the critical eye, there was no way I could notice it without wanting to, how did you put it, judge, discriminate, and evaluate?

That sounds right, he said, but now tell me what was in her eyelashes?

I'll come to it, said his friend, I'll come to it, but let me follow the sequence of events.

All right, so you were in the elevator.

Yes, and it was the longest elevator ride of my life, or maybe from another point of view the shortest, but at any rate we arrived at her floor and she directed me to a suite, and all I could do was follow her exposed legs which I could see beneath all the packages I was carrying, like I said not exactly unattractive, heard the keys jangle and drop and could see more of her come into my little view bending down to collect them slowly, and then we were in the suite with its different lighting and my arms were trembling under the weight of all those packages and...

And?

And it's strange, never happened before or since but I suppose I lost consciousness for there was nothing but the weight and the call of duty to return to the door and the fact of her there, seemingly enjoying this inner conflict of mine, all of it at once made something give.

And?

He met his friend now at the midpoint of this *ad hoc* bridge which had momentarily appeared across the schism. His friend looked away briefly and admitted coming to without a stitch on, the first thing to be seen his uniform neatly folded as though freshly laundered, ironed, and buttons polished, on an armchair nearby the bed in which he found himself lying, the next thing to be seen the reflection of himself in what were remarkable silver eyelashes.

After a pause he said so there was nothing in them at all, save the image of yourself.

That's right.

And then what did you do?

Why, his friend said with surprise at the question, I returned to my watch.

He and his friend began laughing in a way they had not for many years, laughing and laughing.

All right, he said at last, I take your point and shall hereafter refer to a given doorman's tour as his watch, but your account of the night you left the door fortifies my dissertation with a serviceable illustration, seeing as the person for whom you held open the door that night was unknown to you and yet you held open the door for her.

Yes.

Why?

I already said, his friend retorted, she had keys and was a lady, so I assumed.

Excuse me, he interrupted his friend, but you did not assume, you placed faith.

In her?

Opening the door was an act of faith, as it always is when you hold open the door for anyone, especially a stranger, faith in their deserving that act.

Then the critical eye is not paramount?

My thinking hadn't extended to any certainty on such a point, he confessed, and I am uneasy at the suggestion, I hope not simply because of pride, but the faculties of apprehension may well be integral to the manifestation of this central faith.

I see what you mean, his friend nodded, and will have myself to reconsider the relation of duty to faith.

He winked at his friend and replied but it is I who must be thankful to you for illumination, for your telling me about the night you left the door throws my dialectical top for another unexpected spin, that is, more than the relation between acts of duty and acts of faith, what is the difference between an act of faith and an act of love?

His friend looked a little sad and said it may be, my friend, that there are things even beyond the understandings of a doorman.

The greenhouse effect

Count to ten, my mother used to advise, though it was impossible to say whether it was for her benefit or mine. Whenever you feel yourself growing angry, slowly count to ten.

1.

The first time I let it go. Entirely, or almost entirely, let it pass. It was not difficult to imagine your position: young, newly introduced to boredom, and shortly thereafter to opportunity. Botany, I perhaps ought to explain right from the start, is thought by many people to be in fact not worth thinking about – some might admit, when lightly pressed, that the enterprise seems *dull*. Dull? Oh, watching seeds and plants grow and all of that, knowing your stamen from your hymen, very important and very current I know, we need to understand the environment more these days what with global warming and the greenhouse effect, but not one of the more *dramatic* sciences, is it? Accompanied by a friendly grin, even a high laugh from someone nearby. And I defer, inevitably, You may have a point there. In the particular instance in my mind's eye the man who may have had a point had his third drink in hand and was, as well as I can recall, tall and flushed with Scotch health, somewhere in the better part of his thirties. Only the once. I met him once, a lukewarm party in May, which I left early with indigestion, not of course unaware which way the wind was blowing. (That's another of my mother's expressions.) You may have a point, said I, the botanist. I could explain, I could give a detailed rejoinder, a discordant ode to plant life, but instead the good-humoured shrug. To explain how destiny is written in the bloom of an iris, the weed's resilience, and the poetry of photosynthesis would require me to stoop, and I choose never to stoop.

2.

Whether my silence, the very silence of plants, represents a failure, or some weakness of character, is frankly not a question which has much interested me. Recriminations are the sometime occupation of brutes in their idle moments. Consider the pure deliberation of the tree reaching to embrace its immodest lover, the sun: no harmful consternation deters its stolid growth, its truly inner strength. There was an oak whose composure I used to envy in my childhood home's long backyard. For weeks after my father's death I often used to commune with it – or attempt to – for entire afternoons. In part this activity was a retreat from my mother's almost constant jeremiads. You hate to hear about my family, I know, but I am trying to explain. I knew about the first and said nothing, expressed nothing, but the words added up waiting to come out in time in a rush. Even the second, a more prolonged matter that stretched through the fall that year, went without much comment (from me if not among others on the campus), though maybe my silences themselves, my devotion to my studies, late into those nights, were intended as a signal. Patience was the virtue extolled by the oak: that's what those inner concentric rings of biography counsel. Slowly count. They did not tell me to be hopeful, though I'm afraid I was, a little.

3.

Dinner we used to share all the time. Not for long, I grant you, but it was always a pleasure, and though you do not believe me it is a pleasure now. Just the window there, reminding of the unpleasant wet evening from which the warmth of being inside and together protects us, makes dinner that much more satisfying an experience, for the sense of relief it evokes. It was a mild February like this one, do you remember, when we first met. I was in the last semester of my Bachelor's and you were taking a life-drawing class down the street from the lab. You were sobbing with a portfolio case clutched in your lap, sitting by that sculpture I could never make sense of and, to cheer you up, I asked you what you thought it was supposed to be. Do you remember? You said, How should I know, and then just kept on crying, so we went for coffee so at least you could cry where it was warm. The instructor, you cried, had flatly declared you without talent. As someone who understands nothing of art, I scanned the pages attentively but with no certainty, except for my enthusiasm at a male nude in charcoal which reminded me very much of a thriving *Cactacaea fulvinanus*. Only when I ordered you another cappuccino did your eyes dry. They have stayed dry, actually, ever since that time. It was my mother who took up the tears. Announcing the engagement was in prospect a horror, but in execution a strange thrill. My mother burst apart at the seams. Your father made such a mistake, giving it to you directly like that. You have no understanding of money and even less of people, she said, or shouted. Clear mental pictures of a ring, a golden vine, deflected her words. It was a summer afternoon, the first time I had ever confronted my mother and stood my ground, and for days after that I was delirious with something like freedom, made all the more dizzying for my pulse's new rhythm. Dinners were special, when we talked and when we didn't, and I saw no one, no one else but you, though by the time of the third I began to notice how much I was not noticing.

4.

Where anger did not work, my mother found in disease more functional levy. I had to spend much time with her, though she spoke little other than to complain, and as the months went on the messes I had to clean became more size-able and frequent, so many specimens went unheeded but calmly grew and endured, and the fourth, a weekend jaunt as far as I can figure, happened (I nearly said came and went) without much ado. We were no longer dining together, and spooning to mother was no substitute. Her aspidistra seemed to sigh audibly when I was alone with it, but the precise source of its despair was not for me to know. It may be that despair is just that: not knowing what it is that holds you in its grip.

5.

We spoke across this same table at the time of the fifth, and unlike now you then had much to say. Perhaps you remember the exchange better than I do, but it left me unable to leave the table until dark, long after you had gone. There was little denial, some evasion, but a lot of blame. My inade-quacies were served up like part of the meal, each dish colder than the last. Your accusations show how little you trust and value me, you said. They show how little you are. (This matter of being little became a theme.) And so predictable, you know nothing, your crazy puking mother is right about one thing, you know nothing about money, nothing about people, noth-ing about nothing. (The fact that the fifth was a doctoral can-didate in the English department seemed to have little enough effect on your rhetoric.) The barbs kept coming. Obsessed with money. Not concerned enough with your happiness. Inattentive to financial issues. Always talking. Ignorant of the world of feeling. Fixated on how you spent your every moment. Frittering away money and then moaning about it. Never saying anything. And botany! What kind of profession was that for a man? *Plants!* With a crash that I knew was the spiteful murder of a kitchen rhododendron of many loyal years, you left for the night, and in the later half-glow of dusk in the dining room I realized I was halfway to anger.

6.

Mother died at last that spring, and a family which had before seemed negligible in number exploded into a mob uniformly in black and all very pushy with their commiserations. Bereavement softened the usual routine, so that botany was shortly assessed as interesting, full stop, and I could agree no differently than when it was dull or worse, though there was plenty of this agreeing to do – by which I mean, I'm ashamed to say, that there was enough time taken up in my doing so. Of the sixth I know nothing other than that he was at least not a direct relative. (When you listen to it, there is an inherent meanness to the way the number is pronounced, *six*, like a hiss. The resentment is built into the word.) Where's Daphne, she must be so distressed, they said, and I agreed, with words other than my customary, You may have a point, but words with the same meaning. Yes, she must be. It has been very difficult – that *that* was actually difficult to say despite or because of its being true made my collar contract even more tightly around my poor, oxygen-dependent throat. Bad taste, I began to think, and as you've taken opportunities to point out, discernment of such things is not among my stronger abilities. (Bad taste: that is an interesting and rather relevant phrase. But when did I become so interested in the turns of words? Does it come of storing them up, incubating them like hothouse flowers?) The uneven desk leg upstairs was audible as I kept my gaze lowered and felt real sorrow for the holocaust of flowers ostensibly displayed for my comfort. Why these massacres for shows of meagre feeling on our parts? Let no plants be presented at my end save those which of their own will entwine my carcass in the soil!

7.

I especially love begonias, he said, though I doubt I would know one from a South California fiddlehead.

There's no such thing as a South California fiddlehead, I said.

He looked at me with pity – he was not that much younger than I, though he made a great show of his virility in his manner and dress – and said, after a pause, Well, you would know.

I would know. Did the three of us laugh? I don't remember.

8.

Unless I'm mistaken, the eighth lasted the longest. By then I was numbering merely, and took little notice of genus and specimen details of your cultivations, but even so this case was exceptional enough for me to expend more effort in interested observation. His name, Pfander, was only one of the exotic features continuously displayed. Word about the new visiting professor in the Modern Languages department spread quickly, though not for his credentials. Athletic in form but never found near a gym, a favourite among students for his political remarks and flexible due dates, Pfander was a darling of the dean that year and the dean was not alone in his tastes though others savoured the taste in other ways. Lean and loved Pfander once gave a lecture, you might remember it but will be surprised to hear I was in attendance – as I said, I was curious – about the need to revolutionize curricula. The revolution seemed to be against traditions such as giving particulars. Questions were *fielded*, I noticed, if not *answered*. But I cannot be too critical, for partway through the period of raised hands the image of them gently waving and the sound of the word *field* brought on a transformation of the scene. Beanstalks all around me in this reverie, the cool music of the wind promised resolution and a renewed avowal of camaraderie. How long this experience lasted I don't know, but when the hall reasserted itself my gaze was met by that of the Pfander-smitten dean, who had just decided what fields to cut down in his newly inspired reforestation plans.

9.

The same cancer, my mother's cancer: what are the odds? (No, I will not complicate my simple counting with statistical digressions.) For a time it looked as though – in no small part because of the eighth's disappearance – things would settle down when the news came, for it offered a change of roles. But novelty cannot compete with a handsome oncologist. Grimly I now and again wondered if he had bothered to switch off his flashlight between respective searches and examinations. He was very seasoned, and liked to tell me that his wife was a gardener. Maybe you can put her mind at rest, he said. I very much doubted that. It's this buzz about the "greenhouse effect," he said, pronouncing the quotation marks. Molly wonders, you know, how it will affect her marigolds and whatnot. It's a gradual phenomenon, I explained with as much aplomb as someone can in the posture I was in. I suggested a couple of books, and said, Awareness and faithful preparation can avert the worst troubles.

10.

Though the tenth began in December and reached its climax in January, I waited until February, for the sake of the name. You would look puzzled if you were listening to me now, but I wonder if you listened when you could, when you did not because it might have seemed, for lack of a better word, dull. There was a time, long before I began counting to ten, back when I had not thought there might be any counting at all (and on that count I was the insensible one), when I spoke to you of a *Daphne mezereum*, pretty daughter of the *Thymelaeaceae* family. Nature and irony are the same thing. You never were much of a listener, I think, though the crushed seeds in your salad, mixed of course with other selections, appear to have changed that – long enough, that is, for me to count your ten.

The Annotated Affair

What do you cry about?
What? I don't cry.
In your sleep, you make sounds.

I don't cry, he says, not testily but plainly. *In the prison they sewed up my tear ducts.*

Rising from the yard next door, shrieks and a small dog's bark: the pig-tailed girl has thrown up from the cake, and a boy is delighting in having told her so. The sounds are cut by the adult organizers of the party, who take the girl inside for a debriefing before her mother is cautiously telephoned. This may be sticky as the mother[659] is a known dogmatist when it comes to matters of nutrition.

You must want *to cry. The sounds...*

What Winters says next will surely be important – clutch the pencil – but then, oh, he says nothing. He is silent, and Brynn is obviously trying to think of what to say. She has tact, though. Even when they come together (twice a week, roughly; but sometimes more) there are only the sounds of breath and fabric, and the noiselessness of sweat merging. Talking comes later, but precious little of it. What comes must be savoured. Their longest conversation, from the first time, was of the weather, of all things:

It's growing cold, he says. He has to be referring to the outside. *That's something I like here.*

It's not that cold. Only September.

---

659 Mrs. Cauliflower (*see Notebook 4*).

It will get colder. Certainty in his voice. *Winter is good to me*.[660]

Then they talked of the scars which punctuate his body's terse grammar. Brynn wants to know what they mean; Winters speaks in abstractions, tells her when he paints her house he thinks of painting *her*.[661] Brynn has a pleasant chuckle; everybody who meets her seems to like it.

Do that again.

Do what again?

(Do what again?)

That.

* * *

I am Next Door. My place is clean, and I take an unshakable pride in that, though I doubt anybody would generally characterize me as proud. My appearance, for example, is not worth mentioning: just a weathered mop of white hair sitting on top of a gigantic set of fishbowl glasses and a toothless mouth. My sight you might describe as poor and I would thank you for it, but don't fool yourself thinking those books there are for show. Yes, I was a great one for reading when I could, and it always makes me smile when someone scans my little bookshelf and says, "Anthropology? That's like pyramids, yeah? You've read about anthropology?" As though a woman could not understand so many syllables. I give them my Nice Old Lady Smile Number Four; the one that says *you've caught me out in another one of my romantic delusions, but let me keep it anyway,*

---

660 Hence the name. Brynn's name is Brynn Elizabeth (?) Duncanson.

661 Sub- and urban lifestyles of the late twentieth century have strangely inverted traditional courtship rituals. Note here that the significant "singing of praises" figures only as a post-coital gesture. Experience, or consummation, is not earned (climax), but rather serves as the test (crisis).

you kind soul. The Seven Smiles are the most powerful tool an elderly person possesses, and also, because of this, the most secret. Captives of seniors' homes are to be pitied for their ignorance of this arcana. Just a simple appreciation of Smile Number Three, one of the most subtle of the Smiles, might have saved them the disgrace, if employed correctly. Well, that and a little bowel control, I suppose.

My eyes are such that I could not reread the heavy volumes on my little bookshelf even if I wanted to, but there are my ears to rely on. I hear everything. And besides, the only things I read now are the occasional cards from grandchildren and, of course, the Notebooks. If one were to discover the Notebooks in their hiding spot, a quick look at the large script within would reveal the extent of my vision's decline. (This has happened, I fear to report: a woman from a magazine whose title sticks only to a memory uncluttered by thought "dropped in" to ask a few questions of me as a female university graduate who had never been granted a degree because of said femaleness. "Are you angry, or bitter?" "Oh *no*, dear." "*I* would certainly be angry. You *worked* for that degree. As hard as any man." "It was a different time," I said, and noticed with horror that the current Notebook was resting in plain view on the coffee table; whereupon she noticed my looking at it and picked it up. Her carefully trimmed nails slid through the pages – but, thank the forces that be, she was looking, not reading. "You keep a diary?" I told her what she obviously wanted to hear: Oh, just a few notes over the years...a quick dose of Nice Old Lady Smile Number Four...nothing that would interest anybody else... Had I thought of autobiography? I may have gone too far in treating the word as foreign to me, but she went along with it as it led her to the conclusion she had hoped for. And her article dwelt on my modesty, the saintly characteristic of one so hard done by. In any event, the lesson to hide the Notebooks was learned.)

This insert is itself assuming too autobiographical a tone,

though I would chalk up such mild self-reflexivity to a good understanding of the anthropologist's awareness of his or her presence and accompanying effects within the framework of any observation or experiment.

* * *

There is a lot of sex in October and November, which is not untypical with Canadians.[662] He does not come at Christmas, however, and the question of his marital status remains stubbornly a question. Brynn has skated around this issue on occasion. (1) In the last moments of their second time together:[663]

Do you live alone?

No, he says. *I can't afford it, doing work like this.*

I suppose not. (She must feel foiled: this is said in the same tone in which she sighs at an empty mailbox.) She changes tact: *There's a lot of work to be done with this place. More than just painting.*

Hm. A characteristic noise: is he thinking or is he thoughtless?

(2) Between coital activities (the second bout of significant duration), early one evening:[664]

They're calling for snow [665] She pauses, and clicks on a bedside lamp. *I like walking in the snow, except alone. Then it makes me feel terribly alone, just me against all of those billions of individual snowflakes. If I were a decent woman, you could take me for a walk*

---

662 See Appendix B for exact dates and general pattern of frequency; for comparison see H. R. Meridian's somewhat faulty survey in the summer 1977 number of *Human Relations*.

663 The afternoon of September 14, 1990.

664 October 9, 1990.

665 "They" (colloquial): a common usage for authorities; in this case, popular meteorology reporters. Forecasts, while not held as altogether reliable in this period, constitute a makeshift universal reference point. See my earlier observations on horoscopes (*Notebooks 2 and 5*).

one evening when it really starts to snow.

What would your neighbours say, you walking with me?[666] He chuckles. His chuckle is not like Brynn's: it is somehow wrinkled with experience.

The subject drops, and moans arise.

* * *

Despite my age (and I will not add "and perhaps failing senses," or any such bilge), I am not altogether insensitive to the vitality and warmth, if I may put it so, of the situation. Nor to the need of privacy, if I may add that. Some cultures – and I use the term in both the biological and anthropological senses – can only be observed covertly, as their development may depend to varying degrees upon the idea of isolation or "nonobservability."

A brief anecdote (though perhaps it is just as much a confession) inserted here may humanize the analyst's gaze. As an undergraduate, so many years ago, when women were not undergraduates, I did experience love in a deep and moving way. (Ah, Professor Henry, do you think of me?) It will be entirely up to history (or, at least, biographers) to determine to what extent emotionally charged events shape a scientific vision, but whether Professor Henry's ultimate decision not to divorce his myopic, steatopygous wife of nine years for someone who was fresh in mind and warm to[667]

* * *

January 16, 1991. And then, expected and unexpected, *la fin de l'affaire*:

---

666 Michel Foucault's unoriginal label of us as "other Victorians" applies to more than sexuality – also to courtship and its observances.

667 [*Hiatus in MS*]

He visits early in the morning, which is something new. Without his painting gear. Chairs in the kitchen slide on the floor: they sit down, presumably with coffee. After much murmuring – non-coital – there is Brynn's voice, *No, you don't need to.*

More undecipherable words are exchanged.[668] He says in a gentle voice, *The shrine laments, the bedroom weeps, wherein we used to perform the wedding rites. The courtyard is in grief, the storehouses sob, wherein we used to perform the rites of mutual love.*

What's that?

A type of poem...translated. A very, very old poem. He talks as if of an old, stale joke.[669]

She says nothing at first, but her breathing is forceful, a kind of reproach in itself.

You're just using it as an excuse. Why should they want you now? You're not afraid.

I used to have a family, he says.[670] A longer silence, and then: *I'm sorry.*

And he leaves only disappointment behind.[671]

---

668 Possible words used (from impressions, possibly misheard) include (i) Winters's "sorry," "insane" (twice), "the agency" (twice), "hunted"; and (ii) Brynn's "last," "bush," "touch me." Unfortunately the unexpected presence of a plumber problematized observation methods, but the exchanges which follow were noted after the plumber finally, if reluctantly and rudely, agreed to return another day.

669 [Note in progress:] Poetry also out of synch with courtship? – further paradigm reversal in casual love – "Dear John / Jane" as verse (?). See note 651.

670 See preliminary adultery study of Mr. Mull and Ms. Chordstruck (*Notebook 2*).

671 See conclusions to the four case studies in the first Notebook, as well as supporting evidence collected in the opening to the third. I have elsewhere commented on the flaws of previous studies in this area, particularly on those in H. R. Meridian's 1975 book, *Breaking Up: Paradigms and Problems* and in his many subsequent interviews on the subject (*see Notebook 3*).

Doubt's Dream

By this time their arguments had become intolerable. Although they did not shout – Volus stored a little pride in the fact that he could count on one hand the number of times in his life he had raised his voice – the hostility festered at the room temperature a civil volume may afford such an infection, and when they passed each other, he and his wife did not touch. He found the effort of avoiding one another was exhausting, but if she shared the feeling, she did not show it, and it was only when she went to bed that Volus knew he could climb the stairs to the studio and get some work done, undisturbed.

One morning, after having worked yet another long night through, he washed his face and stood back, as he had done so many times before and certainly with no greater expectations than at those moments, to look at what the light would judge. On this morning, however, he was amazed and bounced out of his studio to the windows, into the hallways, at each turn crying out:

A new colour! I've invented a new colour!

That the neighbours did not respond avidly to these alarms testified in more or less equal parts to their generally lethargic disposition as well as to their enthusiasm-dampening familiarity with this dreamer who called himself an artist. It was always something; although, as one swarthy digger was the first to say, this was a new one at least. And he was making a racket, that was unusual, too. Yes, said the digger, intrigued enough to put down both shovel and canteen, usually he just goes on about the current painting, it's coming along, oh yes, coming along, or else it's I've run into an interesting problem, to do with the composition you see, oh it's difficult but it's interesting, takes all of my time, can't dig today. Some weakly chuckling, as at a joke that is too old to be sacrificed, this digger and a few others began to make their way towards Volus, who had by this time emerged into the square. He had a better grip on his excitement, or maybe just had run out of breath from running, but in any case he was speaking with a little more control.

I'm sorry about all the, the noise but, you heard me, you heard, it's amazing you have to see it, I've invented a new colour.

The handful of people who had come to meet him in the square blinked in the morning light. Where's your wife? one of the diggers asked Volus, after no one had said anything.

Now it was Volus's turn to blink. She's probably in bed, I don't know.

Another digger, given to prurient suggestions to disguise his own puritan's insecurities, raised an eyebrow and remarked that a husband who doesn't know if his wife's in bed first thing in the morning has invented nothing new at all. There's already a colour for that situation, the digger said, and there was some general laughter before a cook, often censorious in public though rather wanton in private thoughts, put in that a wife showed a lot of sense staying alone in bed when married to an irresponsible husband. You want to make her a happy colour, the cook said, you do some honest work. For this interruption the digger gave the cook a wink, earning a cold look in return; but the digger would later alone rue the gesture and the cook alone dream of its potential.

Volus said, you must come see, it's in my studio, but it was too late; he had been dismissed and everyone was returning to work. Oh, yes, come to my studio, we've heard it before, it's always come look come see, it's coming along. Volus's protests that this was different, that he had done something different, were not heeded. There's digging to do; there's cooking to get done.

This refrain was as old and cavilling for bleary-eyed Volus as his implications were old and irritating to his neighbours. He surrendered himself to the stairs. For the first time in what might for a lark be called memory, he thought of his wife as a locus for hope. Songs they almost danced to years ago gradually came back to his ears, but they merged together into one very uneven song whose simple lyrics when forced into close congress began to grow warped and contradictory together. Even whistling this new song would involve chewing on one's tongue. Moving to the bedroom, he began his address in as calm a manner as he could:

Vina, dear, you must see. You will not believe it, Vina, my songbird, but something amazing has happened. I hardly believe it myself, and of course those idiots of neighbours don't believe anything that cannot be shovelled, but you, Vina, you, my darling, you.

But the bedroom was empty and no one was listening; the next room and the next room were likewise without Vina and still no one was listening. The unusual sense of disappointment that came with this discovery was made worse by the fact that the disfigured medley he had summoned now attained a firm grasp on his mind. He ran back down the stairs and outside into the square again, where a few neighbours were milling about, comparing accounts of drudgery.

Have you seen Vina? he asked them. Has anyone seen my wife?

Now that's a strange thing to be asking, someone said, seeing as that's just what we were asking you this morning. Another pursed fat lips and mimicked Volus with no real talent: I've invented a new colour, I'm an artist, I can't dig, I'm a painter, I can't cook, really, I've invented a new colour now, come see, come see. Proving that the neighbourhood had no shortage of comedians, a third voice cut through the subsequent laughter to add in an even more feeble imitation, I've found a colour but I've lost my wife. More likely she's come to her senses, a fourth responded, and left him in the night. Many is the time we've heard her complaints and all of us nodded with heavy head, many is the time she heard our complaints and nodded with heavy head, and the complaints always the same. Doesn't dig, doesn't cook, what good is he. Good for nothing, said a fifth, who had been waiting for some time to chime in, even if he has invented a new colour, who needs another colour anyhow.

This last remark brought Volus renewed conviction and silenced the racket in his head. I have invented a new colour, he said hotly, and I want my wife to be the first to see it. She'll understand it, she has a discerning eye. It's too splendid an invention for any of you to appreciate. You only know the colour of filth.

One of the more truculent diggers stepped towards him and said, Listen here, filth has many colours. You might even say there's a wide spectrum in every shovel. Or in every spoonful, added a cook. But when I'm sweating away at it, the digger continued, making pantomime gestures of digging to make his point, you don't hear me disturbing the peace about the fact. I mix a new colour every day, the cook rejoined with a stirring motion.

Volus's fire had faded. What was his new colour, what made it new, what made it different from what was unearthed and broiled by these neighbours? He realized that it had been hours since he had last slept, that the mind blurs things, like those songs he and Vina had never quite danced to, that there was a chance, a dim possibility. And so doubt now entered his mind, which was in no shape to receive any more guests today. Had he truly invented a new colour? he wondered as he went again, much slower this second time, up the stairs to his lodgings. For that matter, he wondered with doubt as they say settling in, was he really any kind of artist at all? Insinuations about his not being right in the head were occasionally heard in the square; even his wife was not above making such suggestions on a more or less regular basis. What if it were true, what if he had been wrong all the time, what if the only colours were those found in cooking and digging, digging and cooking? Now quite comfortable, doubt stretched out its legs, gave out a yawn and muttered, old songs and new colours, before falling asleep.

Volus ascended to the studio, determined to see again, or perhaps see for the first time, or from yet another point of view not see at all the new colour. If it is a new colour, he promised himself before opening his eyes (he suddenly thought, as doubt burbled and twitched in sleep, how all of this could be, could have been, would be a dream when he opened them), if it really is new, I will never argue again with you, my dear, darling songbird. If it is a new colour, our marriage shall be new, if it is new and you ask me never to paint again, I will give up my brushes for a shovel or a spoon as you prefer, if it is new, we will dance together to all of the songs.

He opened his eyes, and met the colour of Vina's.

An Unlikely Sequence

True, between faces almost any number
Might come in handy, and One is always real;
But which could any face call good, for calling
Infinity a number does not make it one.
— W. H. Auden, "Numbers and Faces"

i am, or can be, the square root of negative One. i mean to say, were i to be multiplied by myself (how? Don't ask) i would become One less than Zero. One may, rather understandably, at times, get a little confused by this idea; and this has understandably put something of a strain on my relationship with her.

One begs description. i cannot manage this, however. One is more substantial than my little words; so electrifying with her simple reality and wholeness, unlike the countless others. i am uncertain near her whether i am near her at all, or else i think of her from a distance and it is as though she is near. i suppose i am in love with her, deeply integral and wholly impossible love, unnatural and irrational because to love her, i would have to exist. i am not sure i do, because i am not sure i *am*.

Zero is the real problem – if he is in fact any more real than i am, which i lately doubt. i think perhaps he shares this feeling for One. i suppose that in some way she seems (nay, i know not seems...does, emphatically does) to make those who love her, those who will stand and be counted with her, *more real*. Zero has as a name the precise measurement of his personality. One can't possibly love him. i freeze and leave off blinking when i think of her touching his vacant face and formless figure. Zero's eyes are empty, or else they choose to reflect the emptiness in those who for whatever unfortunate reasons have to look at him. Zero is simply there, feigning significance while dividing One and i.

* * *

i ought to be honest, but i have to be calculating. One may not even know i exist, though we have met many times, always at crowded functions. i don't really enjoy these events – the exaggerated manners and enthusiasms, the ridiculously swollen value of mechanical interactions – but i'm often obliged to make an appearance, mostly to take up social slack or smooth out business operations. i'm basically a troubleshooter. i admit that it's an interesting job and wins me unusual respect, but rewards in friendship are marginal, lost, and usual mere errors in judgement.

One frequently goes to these events. i like to watch her move through the crowd, her generous gestures; her laconic nod of considered agreement. Zero only accompanies her in the way an umbrella goes with somebody when it may chance to rain, and he barely registers the introductions while he conspicuously consumes more than a decent share of the party spread. i have met him too, on these occasions, and have tried to discover whether some buried charm might be glimpsed in conversation. i've found nothing, however. Zero's small talk is more breath than words, and he swings from smugness to self-deprecation too easily to make any certain claims about anything. One's...*oneness*...is diminished somehow by Zero.

Zero suspects nothing. i consider this an advantage as i prepare my overtures to his wife and simultaneous preponderance on his own fate in my scheme. i don't think he can be "cancelled out" or "eliminated" (terminologies fail when discussing this non-entity!) – he is too powerful. Zero's position in our zealous little set is practically unassailable; the idea of killing him unthinkable. One could not love me as a murderer in any case. i know i must find another way.

* * *

i don't know if the ability to dream certifies the reality of the dreamer; after all, who dreams of the Red King? i'm the Knave at best, dreaming of my hands encircling my beloved's knees. (i don't dream of Zero, and can't imagine that anybody does.) One calls out to me in these brief dreams, giving voice to a gorgeous sound I've never heard before but by which i recognize *myself*: it is One's name for me. i love it. i want to hear it again, learn it, be called by it. One may address me this way, tonight, at the party. i am having a party. Zero's invitation has regrettably been lost.

One, a touch late, splendidly scorning fashion, lips pressed in careful observance, indifferent to flattery, graceful, tangible, light and dark, bread and wine, so many things, my world in a nutshell, a touch late, arrives. i will suffer no more separations, no further division. i approach with calm, control, and good humour. "i am i." "One," she says, for there is nothing worth saying after this kind of introduction. i may be i, but One is *One*. One has it together, whereas i most assuredly do not. (Zero has nothing to get together, and so doesn't need to worry about it.) i tell One she has it together, so wonderfully together, with the stammer of the very amateur flirt. One smiles; an awkward pause; and i flatter her again that she's really together. One's smile is pained and i realize a deeper plunge is urgently required. i load the words "i love you" into my vocal crossbow, but then the unwanted cavalry bursts in. Zero crashes my party.

Zero in fact *broke up* my party. i can't understand, let alone describe, how dullness surrounds him like a cloud and stains the air of any new and unsuspecting space he enters. i was suddenly shaking hands again with each of the guests, all of whom had to go, had just remembered an appointment, were feeling tired or unwell or both, and so on. Zero, oblivious, pushed handfuls of fruit and cheese into his ridiculous mouth. One moved to join him, kissing him on the forehead with enough force to crush my hopes – for i saw in that moment the awful necessity of her tenderness. Zero needed her more than i ever could: the slight kiss glimpsed through the traffic of departing guests told me this. i understood then that there is an agreement, an unpalatable logic which binds them together. Zero, with nothing else, must have One.

* * *

i admit, it's not much of a story; but then, i'm not much of a subject. i think the problem is that maybe there is no story, and there is only me. i am the fiction, and the rest is dreadfully real. i have discussed this with my analyst – a very constant man known as Planck – and he tells me that i will never solve these problems. i can only simplify them, change the terms. i know there is no equation for the heart.

Checking

The bird first appeared, or was first seen, on Sunday, in the morning. For some reason or other the violet curtains in the kitchen window aggravated me, that way inanimate objects seem impudent or else simply improper, call for straightening out even though there will be no satisfaction when the rough act is done. It was something they were doing to the sunlight; cheapening it, maybe, or just making it seem dull or sad. I enjoy feeling the sun on my face as much as I do, Dari told me the last time she called, because it takes no effort on my part.

In our backyard in that apartment, the like of which cannot be had now for the rent we paid then, was a fairly large birdbath, one of those cement numbers apparently manufactured to give birds the impression that they were visiting ancient Athens. Until that morning, which adds up to at least eighteen months of residency, I had never glimpsed even a feather in the bath. Now there was this smallish, orgulous being, beak pointed directly at me as though pointing me out to another, unseen bird. It did not move.

It had seen me before I saw it.

Dari was just out of the shower, pacing between bedroom and bathroom wrapped in a couple of unmatched towels. She bicycled every weekday morning and sometimes, more and more often, on the weekends, too. Hard, she said, and it could be felt in her thighs. For the past year and half, when this new and forceful regime of alternating exercise and work took hold, our occasional moments of sex held the most inexplicable feeling for me when I laid my palm across her bicep and then gently squeezed. For some reason this contact with muscle turned me on hopelessly, but just as strangely, also made me just a little sad.

Looking at the bird, I did not call to Dari, to tell her to come see. She was probably preparing, sketching, planning in her mind whatever pitch she was to give the next day, and though she never said so, I know that my interruptions to these thought processes awoke a cool resentment which she would carry and add to until the week had done. There was a lot that was trivial about me, and that once dependably, and now only then and again, worked as a charm.

I found myself wondering where the birdbath had come from, who had bought it and to what purpose (was there a certain kind or class of bird that was anticipated? Was it this very bird staring at me?), how much had it cost. The last question proved the most difficult and I realized as I began to play with numbers that I was avoiding the gaze of the bird, letting my cowardly eye flit around the curve of the pedestal but keeping it from rising any higher. Even worse, when I tried to imagine what reason I might have for projecting who knows what qualities onto this backyard visitor, the question of price reclaimed the forefront of my thoughts. What did the bird symbolize? I don't know, but surely I could guess the value of the birdbath.

– Have you seen my sweater? called Dari. The red one.

I let the curtains fall to make their violet trouble with the light, and picked up the sweater hanging over the back of the nearest kitchen chair. Dari yawned as she took it from me.

– I didn't sleep well last night. I dreamt I was cycling and these men were cycling behind me, trying to catch up.

She sniffed the collar of the sweater and nodded to herself, the way I'd seen her do even in stores before she tried something on. As her head emerged from the fabric, I asked her how much the birdbath in the yard cost.

– Why?

– Curious.

– You are that. The thing that was really vivid about the dream, you know, was the breathing. I could hear all those guys exhaling, like they were really tired or out of shape or something. But I thought they were gaining on me and I had to keep going.

– I'll get your coffee, I said.

Fatalism has never impressed me, and I measure myself a rational sort, though I do sense something like fortune at work sometimes. Dari would not talk about such things, and maybe that refusal has to do with how her brother died. They had been swimming together one afternoon on family holiday in a place called Sacred Sands. I never asked where that was, but for some reason figured it was on a lake in New England somewhere. Dari, almost two years younger than her brother, made it look easy and this frustrated him. They raced, over and over, and she always won. By the last few times, Dari said, she was teasing him pretty badly. Her father actually broke from his catatonic reading of his technical manual – he was an aeronautics expert, and being that took almost all of his time and concentration – to tell her to let her brother alone.

Some time after the other three members of his family had fallen asleep, ten-year-old Neil crept out of the tent and headed down to the water. Dari guessed he had gone to practice his strokes. He would beat her the next day; he was imagining her face when she, winded, found him waiting at the finish line. He was found instead by another camper, a self-confessed early riser. Dari never saw the body, but years later she was given an image when she overheard her mother, wracked by nightmares, sob as if her face were pressed into a pillow, a shoulder, her own sleeve: *all of the colour had been drained out of him.*

More than once I had heard this story, and each time I am sure I disappointed Dari with my not saying what she wanted to hear, but I am also sure she did not know herself what that might have been.

Mondays are always quietest, and I tend to get a lot done then. The bird was there that morning, still looking at me, but this time it was expected – I don't know why, exactly, but he had lost the element of surprise – and I got on with the business at hand. *How many ambidextrous pitchers had there been in the National League?* Sports questions tend to bore me because they so often come to nothing but numbers, statistics without a story. *Is it true that some professional golfers sleep with a ball under their pillow the night before a big tournament?* Even though that's a yes-or-no affair, there's a narrative there. That's the kind I like. The joy of being a Fact Checker (a lower-case job title if ever there were one, but a modicum of self-esteem does make it easier to respond to curious looks) lies in that idea: no matter how unusual the question that comes down the pipe from the editors, the Checker gives reply with the sense of being a polisher of the sky. We are not historians, but we straighten out history's frame, dust off its surface. *How many women have run for public office in the state of California in the past century? Which country has the shortest life expectancy? What was Alexander the Great's favourite colour?* These were my days.

I had already taken care of several baseball-related items and was beaming at the prospect of getting to some minutiae on the life and songs of Diana Ross when the doorbell rang, twice. Assuming it to be just another courier with a receipt for me to sign, I grabbed my pen from the desk and twirled it out of habit when I opened the door.

– I'm sorry to bother you, said the woman standing there, looking like she really was sorry to be on my doorstep. There was a nervous energy that was localized in her legs. She smiled and stopped smiling, maybe thinking better of it. She didn't add to her apology.

– It's fine, I said.

– I know this seems very strange but I have reason to, well, there may be a bird in your backyard.

– In my birdbath, I said, and smiled before adding for no reason at all: Actually, it's not my birdbath, it came with the, it was here before.

She smiled at me again, this time even more briefly, and adjusted her glasses.

– But you are, you do live here, this is your house.

– This half of the house, I'm the tenant, yes. Maybe you're looking for the side door, there's a tenant downstairs in the smaller apartment.

The woman scratched her forehead. Her nose was somehow wrong for her face, it had come from some more serious-looking person without the quick eyes and self-biting mouth. She glanced down at her shoes, runners which looked relatively new.

– The thing is, I have been wanting to see this bird, this particular bird, which may be in your backyard right this moment, for, like, several years. More than I'd like to count, actually.

I described the bird, and she interrupted by grabbing my arm with both hands.

– Can I come in and look at it?

Did it never occur to me to ask what was so special about this bird? True, I rarely get the wildlife kingdom questions and, as a Checker, tend to specialize in history, politics, and pop culture. Once I traded a colleague *What are the four largest birds in Asia Minor?* for *How many restaurants are there in Rome that do not serve pasta?* Ornithology is a weak spot. But still I wonder. This woman waited; she was going to come in and look at the bird through my kitchen window. She had no camera, not even binoculars. She was extremely cute, even with the wrong nose. I did not ask her what kind of bird it was, whether it was rare, or anything.

Naturally, the place was not in any shape for visitors. Dari worked long hours most of the time, leaving me sole but uncomplaining housekeeper. Lately I had been slacking off, but Dari was not around enough to give the fact serious notice.

– It's through here. You can see it through the window.

Even before her hand reached the curtains I was certain the bird would not be there. The movement of her arm was not exactly graceful, but there was a small portion of elegance to it that fascinated me. It was as though she had rehearsed this gesture many, many times, and was determined to get it right but at the same time not to let it appear in any way affected. I was looking at her face when the curtains were moved and the empty bath was exposed. She did not turn to look at me, but asked quietly if it had come before today. Nodding, I let a beat pass, then said:

– May I ask a question?

She was still looking out the window when she said, slowly:

– I have reason to believe that the bird you saw in your yard is my father.

Another beat. Now my stare was on her breasts, which surprised me not for my being rude, which my eyes always are (again, Dari would confirm this), but because I usually am indifferent to breasts. Dari has small breasts, inconsequential tits she used to call them, before she would offer me her lips. Mouths drive me crazy. I have been known to suck elbows, and though I'm not a foot fetishist, I can see where those people are coming from. This mystery woman, alleged daughter of the bird, had textbook-perfect tits, the kind that inspired geometry. They were very immediate, like the bird itself: addressing themselves directly to me.

– I don't see the resemblance, I said.

She let the curtains fall and quickly retraced her steps to the front door. I did not follow, but slid back into my chair at the desk and heard the door close. On the laptop's screen was the question *What is the highest note sung in "Where Did Our Love Go?"*

Dari got in just before ten, ordered pizza, ate on the couch. She was exhausted. A guy at work, somebody I'd not then met, was really riding her proposals. She said he got some enjoyment out of it, and he liked the sound of phrases like *in point of fact* and *for all intents and purposes*. I suggested that maybe he was reacting to the trauma of failing to make the debating team in high school by vigorously overcompensating. I suggested that he hoarded videotapes of parliamentary debates and watched them, secretly, late at night, next to a standing mirror. Dari did not laugh.

She needed to laugh. I wanted her to laugh. I told her about how this woman came to the apartment asking to see if there was a bird in our yard. I made up a strange voice, something from a hoarse munchkin from Oz:

– I've been searching, like, all over the world for this particular bird for several, like, years.

– How old was she?

Late twenties, I guessed.

– She looked winded when the bird wasn't there. Young enough to have hopes dashed, old enough not to make a scene. But I haven't told you the really crazy thing.

– She was in the apartment? Dari asked, moving out of her slouch. You let her in?

The rest of the night was an argument, which reached its climax about twenty minutes after it began when Dari first asked me if the woman (Dari, who was thirty then, called her a girl) was cute. I said that wasn't the point. Then she asked me if I fucked her. Was I fucking around? The anger Dari showed was at least two thirds fatigue and frustration, and now, with the wincing clarity of hindsight, I know that she was lashing out against the *all intents and purposes guy*, whose name is Trevor.

I met Trevor a few months ago, but only two things about him stick with me. One is the way he stood, the way he kept some formulaic stance with a regulated distance between his feet, both planted firmly. What his voice sounds like, how he wears his hair, or what he drinks I don't remember, maybe didn't even notice. We had a pretty uneven conversation, there was another guy with us, at this deck party. The host was an old friend from university, he had known Dari too and so Trevor and I wound up in the same spot. And he told this other guy and me that lately the business stakes had really shot up, things were getting even more competitive. It was all sink or swim, he said.

– And since I can't swim, I'm packing a goddamned life preserver. He made a nod in the direction of Dari, who smiled back from the barbecue.

That's all I remember about Trevor: how he stood, checking the solidity of the earth, and that he said he couldn't swim.

Tuesday I got up from the couch and pretended to be awake. I made coffee, noted the smell of dried sweat but decided against showering. I sat in front of the laptop and began to answer questions. *Is Diana Ross the real name of Diana Ross? How many marriages have the Supremes had between them? "Stop! (In the Name of Love)" appears on how many American movie soundtracks between the years 1980 and 1994? What is Diana Ross's height?*

For someone, this would be important information. I had to trust that instinct.

Dari got her own coffee. She had been crying; she wanted me to see that. She stood in the door of the office where I worked, a room whose floor was as filled with sprawling books as its walls were clothed in post-it notes and cuttings. Eventually, starting low, her voice entered the room and expressed calm, stressed calm, advocated the need for calm.

– We're pulling a muscle, you and I, she said. Pulling and pulling, that's what we're doing. And what's happened? We limp together. We're limping, we're not striding. Life is for striding, going places, getting there, not limping along, tearing at one another, wearing each other out.

She thought a break was needed.

How satisfied was Ross with her portrayal of Billie Holiday in Lady Sings the Blues?

What did I think?

– Do me a favour, I said.

– What's that? She put down her coffee.

What's the most money ever awarded a Diana Ross impersonator?

– Go look out the kitchen window and see if there's a bird in the birdbath, looking in at you.

Dari asked why, and picked up her mug again. I said that if it wasn't there, we had nothing to talk about.

Circumstances don't necessarily dictate what happens but you can let them. That's not fatalism. It's like loosening your grip on the steering wheel, letting your fingers just slide against the circumference as it moves. Or it may be like the moment a swimmer has, when he is over his head and tired, and he lets the tide have its way.

Plot

Speak to me that, which spoken, will array me
In its own only precious ornament.

– Wallace Stevens

I

Here is a room. In the room there is a person with tired eyes, staring and then not staring and then staring again at a switch on the opposite wall. The switch is the only feature of the room: no doors, no windows, no furniture.

What follows is a story. In one version of the story, the most popular one, the person crosses the room and throws the switch, and something happens. In another version, less popular but still well-liked, especially among the young, the person crosses the room and throws the switch, but nothing happens. A similar-minded but notably different version has the person cross the room but, for whatever reason, the person is physically unable to throw the switch. Although it seems very like the previous version, throwing the switch but nothing happens, this version of the story, trying unsuccessfully to throw the switch, has a following among the very old.

And then there is the version in which the person does not try to throw the switch. This version is not popular at all. Part of the problem is the story's length, which is a strange point of contention, since there is disagreement about whether it is too short or too long, though it is widely agreed that it is one or the other.[1] But generally there is little discussion about this version

---

1 There was a more severe reaction, some years back, when a militant Member of Parliament rallied to have this version of the story declared unpatriotic. Newspapers noted the campaign in back-page columns for a brief period.

of the story: most people seem to tend to drift back to one of the other versions.

The people who most enjoy the most popular version of the story usually hold that its best element is the switch, or at least the throwing of the switch, because, they contend, it is the switch or at least the throwing of the switch which causes whatever happens to happen. And sometimes some of these people add, as an afterthought, that they identified with the person in the room. On the other hand, those people who prefer the version in which nothing happens when the person throws the switch tend to be less clear in their reasons for their preference, although they do really like the switch, too, or at least the throwing of the switch. About the person in the story there is more ambivalence; and only slightly more so than in the attitudes held toward the person in the version in which the switch cannot be thrown, despite the attempt.

For these reasons mercantile planners tend to seize upon what characteristics they perceive in the person in the most popular version of the story, and try to incorporate them in their market schemes. What came slowly at first but then with eruptive speed were countless commercial slogans about doing things, being active, striving, moving, going, and, in less imaginative instances, throwing switches. Such campaigns tend to be successful still, though to be sure there are lulls – short periods where, usually in the face of some troubling recent event, the public wells for optimism at least appear to be dry. For these short periods of loss and quick recuperation, one or the other of the versions of the story in which the person at least attempts to throw the switch, the ones in which nothing does happen as a result, usually experiences a slight but noticeable swell in popularity. Depending on how traumatic or extended these periods are – in the cases of war or large natural disaster, they can be comparatively enduring – there may be even further changes to the way the story is told. There have been ephemeral versions of the story in which the person throws the switch and something happens, but what happens is so dreadful that it seems all out of proportion with what is, after all, the simple business of throwing a switch. Mercantile planners have had little use for this version of the story. When these lulls occur, some advertising campaigns advance nostalgia as a redemptive quality: Remember, dear heart, when the switch was thrown and something happened, something not dreadful, perhaps something lovely? While such campaigns are never as successful as the usual capitalization on the story of the person throwing the switch, some of them have carried the day; at least, until the lull subsides and the most popular version of the story inevitably returns to vogue.

II

There's another story, or a story that's a continuation of one of the versions of the first story: in these instances, this other story often results from or follows the most popular version of the first story, the one in which the person throws the switch. This next story, if it is connected, artificially or naturally, may be the something which happens when the switch is thrown; but not necessarily.

In this other story, there is another room, or the same room, with another person in it, or else the same person.[2] However, there is another person in the room: that is, an entirely new and other person not taken from some other story. The story is that these two persons are together in this room.

As with the other story, or the part of the story that may follow this later part, there are divergences according to different

---

2 If it is a new room it may or may not have things like doors, windows, furniture, or a switch. There is some minimal difference in popularity between the version of the story in which the room has these accoutrements and the version in which it does not, usually in the favour of the former version.

tastes. Again, one certain version is by far the most popular. In this version, the first person who may be from a previous story is in the room with the other entirely new person and something happens. Interestingly, the majority of those who enjoy the most popular version of the first story also enjoy this version of this story. In fact, this version of this story may be even more popular than the most popular version of the first story. For this reason mercantile planners have had a longstanding love affair with this version of this story. Commercial slogans and scenarios concerning meeting others, interacting, communicating, and generally not being alone are even more popular than those concerning doing things, being active, striving, moving, going, and throwing switches. Especially successful have been advertisements featuring hybrids or combinations of these story versions: for example, a person strives to meet another person, or after throwing a switch, a person encounters another person.

However, the version of the story in which nothing happens between the two people in the room proved almost entirely untenable for commercial use.[3] This version does have its adherents, but many of them are not very communicative about it, and discussions on the matter typically leave frustrated those parties who prefer the more popular version of the story, where something happens when the person encounters the other person.

Some marginal argument continues about whether there may in fact be another version of this story, in which the person in the room encounters another person and something almost happens. Both those who dismiss this variation as an illusion and those who make claims for it seem to be in weak agreement that the potential for something happening, the condition for "almost," has to do with the length of the story,

---

3 An advertising campaign which centred on the idea of a person in a room with another person, where each person seemed unaware of the other, puzzled consumers to such an extent that surveys reported many felt "alienated" and "uncertain."

but there is no agreement as to whether its length is directly or inversely proportional to this potential.

III

Finally, there is yet another story, or a story that's a continuation of one of the versions of the first and/or the second story, if it is assumed that this other, third story is a consequence of the most popular versions of either or both of the other stories, the one in which the person throws the switch, or the person encounters another person, and something happens. Again, though, this story is not necessarily connected to those other stories in such a causal way; and, most unusual of all, there is some contention about whether this story is in fact a story at all.

Here is a room. There may or may not be doors, windows, furniture, or even a switch in this room, depending on the version of the story under way.[4] It may or may not be the same room as the room in either or both of the other stories.[5]

Considerations of whether this is in fact a story are matched by those of whether the story has any variations, which perhaps it ought to if it really is a story. Strangely, as unpopular as this story is, it has never completely faded away,

---

4 It has been pointed out that those versions of this story in which the room does feature a switch are on the whole rather baroque renditions, since the switch is both unnecessary decoration and a misleading connection to the story with the person in the room with the switch.

5 The fact that the room has no person in it has been understood by many to mean that the room in this story is not even comparable to the story in which the person is in a room with a switch or to the story in which a person in a room encounters another person, despite superficial resemblances such as doors, windows, furniture, or a switch. (*See note 4 above.*)

and perhaps even more strangely, mercantile planners have never fully given up on it as a possible source for commercial ideas. Numerous disastrous advertising campaigns notwith-standing, every so often attention comes back to this story of a room – usually in the midst of one of the lulls in interest in the most popular stories – and more than one mind studying the problem has been lost. One strong speculation on the matter holds that this story is very easy to remember, and may yet prove serviceable for that unexploited quality.

In the meantime

Once upon a time (the problem with which introduction becomes self-evident in due course), a young flirt slid, palms against lovely lower shins, towards the unsuspecting sun. However – here the dip into the melody of plot – the star was spared unwanted misery when she happened to catch sight of the most elegant eye she had ever seen, as it blinked at her perfectly from within the dull collection of emptiness.

The distance was so great between her eye and this one that its colour was wholly impossible to discern correctly, though fancy might paint it blue, most blue. (The problems with this sentence are so multi-fold they will have to be ignored, and possibly told in another story altogether. Never mind the conjecture about colour, which would have so faded by Anno Domini 1637 so as not to be "most" anything.)

At any rate.

She swerved from the star because she saw an eye. This unexpected change of pattern actually disappointed the star, who had been blazing away bored at a young age, for at least two fairly good reasons. The first reason was, well, this flirt *was* cute, no denying it really. The second reason was just an extension of the first: even stars get lonely. Any attention at all, as far as this star was concerned, was welcome – and lately there had been a feeling that, indeed, someone was watching; someone down there where this cute stellar flirt was headed. It is heartbreaking to see one of one's few admirers turn to the other with interest.

All of which brings us to Myron. As his name suggests, he

was a failed poet. He was a failure, though, unlike other failures, in the scope of his failed attempts. He was in his time a failed medical student, failed architect, failed politician, failed salesman, failed farmer, failed Catholic, failed sinner, failed ditch-digger, failed fisherman, and failed layabout. His face was obscenely scarless, pink, and tight, and he walked like a child lost in a winding fantasy.

At the moment when the stellar flirt, whose lack of a proper name makes this narrative that much more obstreperous, appeared tapping at his workshop window, Myron was in the middle of a sigh.

– Hello, I saw a beautiful eye. Can you direct me to it?

– I am busy just now, said Myron.

She rudely opened the window and squeezed inside, but Myron pretended not to mind.

– What are you doing?

He wordlessly snatched up a large blueprint from his bench and handed it to her with a good go at contempt. She looked with curiosity at the crudely drawn but elaborate design:

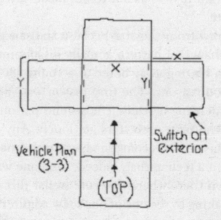

Vehicle Plan
(3-3)

Switch on
exterior

(TOP)

– Wow, she said.

Myron smiled warily. If she only knew.

– And you propose to build this?

– Propose? He said the word like it was from an enemy language. I am building it. Nearly finished, in fact.

The workshop, a ramshackle garage without a car or other purpose, was a careful disorganization of tools, tool-like objects, and unworkable lamps. What it lacked in colour it made up for in mustiness. A dust-laden tape deck was mutedly playing, for anyone who would listen, a Fats Domino collection. However, the most prevalent stuff in Myron's compressed universe was, without contest, cardboard. Masses of cardboard cuttings, broken boxes, leaned and piled and stood and idled.

– And then? she asked. She had never seen cardboard before.

– And then what?

– I mean, and then are you going to use it?

Myron allowed himself his record second smile within a month.

– Where did you say you saw this eye?

She pointed:

– Up there.

Myron squinted at the sky through the open window, though it was not that bright. Why should he believe this girl? She could be a spy; but then there was the bleak hope she could be a companion, an ear, someone to replace Sagredo. Someone to throw the switch.

– You're from down here.

– Yes, he said distractedly. I suppose it's no better up there.

– Better? she asked. How do you mean?

– You say you're from up there, he said with a hoisted thumb, but his eyes down on a large, bent sheet of cardboard. That's your story?

– I just came from there. The eye belongs down here. Likely on a full face, she added.

– Well, he said. Well. What are things like up there, then? Everyone is in such a hurry to get up there. Cosmonauts and all. ("Cosmonauts" a word from the same dreadful argot as "propose.") Is it worth it, really?

She thought about it.

– It's like anything else, she said as she played with the hair around her right ear. You get used to it.

This recognition, which she had never so much as glanced at before, there, high upon a most dusty upper shelf of her unusual consciousness, abruptly introduced her to depression, which she had also never experienced before. All those places, all that space, all the things to do in all that space! She had *gotten used to it*. How dreadful that was; how ridiculous. Her career of bouncing around the galaxy, memorizing silly tunes, and flirting with so many dim stars now seemed a waste of – er, a sham. Her interest in the beautiful eye suddenly seemed more important by merit of its unknownness, its disruption to the norm.

Admirably unempathic, droopy-eyed Myron sensed none of this. Instead of paying attention to this distractive intruder, he walked around the waiting cardboard and tools, as he often did, looking for the appropriate point of attack.

– You should try terrestrial existence, he said sourly. You *never* get used to *it*.

In the meantime, the local stars ("local," of course, just another in a series of inappropriate adjectives) were discussing her absence. The sun was explaining she had been in the neighbourhood (no comment) very recently (again, no comment). One star expressed concern: not that he cared for her, um, questionable behaviour, but still, you see how it is, one ought to worry, you see.

– Maybe fell into a black hole, said another star, just looking for that extra risk and thrill. I always said a smartass like that courts trouble. Doesn't matter how pretty the smartass is.

– Don't be so hard on her, a more sanguine star put in. She's harmless. You make yourselves ridiculous worrying about her. You're supposed to be heavenly bodies, for crying out loud: show some dignity and reserve.

– We're just concerned.

– Oh, yes?

– Well, you're so smart, maybe you know what's happened to her.

– As a matter of fact, I've an opinion about that. An educated guess, nothing more, but I'm not about to share it.

– Hear that!

– Ho, high horse on Phoebus's chariot!

There were other heckles. Despite the benefit of centuries, some stars can be pretty immature.

– Full of hot air. You've no idea where she's gone.

– Ho ho!

– I said it was, or rather it is, nothing more than an educated guess.

– Educated, did you get that, said one proletarian-styled star, with a hard squint. So righteous till they supernova, same as the rest of us. Who put you at the top of the Christmas tree, I want to know.

The rest of the stars in the conversation, with their typical aristocratic postures, did not press this particular point, but did continue to harass and goad their tight-lipped counterpart, for a considerable period – say, nineteen or twenty Jovian revolutions (and even that motional measurement isn't genuinely helpful, given the expansion of everything in every direction) – until, at last, they all grew bored, and took instead to chattily comparing sunspots.

In the meantime:

– Do you ever get lonely?

Myron was genuinely startled by the question.

– Not much. Sometimes, I suppose.

He pointed up again, and asked,

– Do you get lonely up there?

She was bent on being the interrogator, however, and overrode his question with her own:

– Do you work all alone?

He nodded, and turned to the shelf where the better part of a bottle of bourbon sat in anticipation of his thirst. Opening it with a strange, far-away expression in his face, he eased himself into a dusty old chair.

– Wasn't always so. I had a sort of assistant for a while. Sagredo.

After taking a swig, he offered the bottle to his curious guest.

– Tell me about Sagredo, she said.

Myron sat back into his chair further than he had ever tried with this chair, and it creaked with surprise at his boldness, but held him. Waving one hand in the air as though drawing something there, while carefully brushing his eyebrow with the other, he began in an unusually clear tone of voice the toasting speech he had always wanted to give.

– Sagredo, helpful and good Sagredo! He had such good ears. See him there, in my memory, a little blurred but still you can make out those magnificent ears, and you can probably tell that those clothes are a little cheap – but never mind that he wasn't much of a dresser. I'm surprised at myself to find I remember him so: I will dignify him, and misremember him wearing something a little more stylish – there. There, you see? Good old Sagredo!

His listener nodded, and wondered whether she could see Sagredo or not. She tried the bourbon, but found it tasteless, and handed back the bottle.

– There are, Myron went on, when I think very finely over the mental territory in question, a discernible number of qualities that made Sagredo so helpful and good, though to be entirely frank, none of them involves his theology, which could charitably be called a confused mess. Part of this disaster, to be sure, was the fault of Simplico, whom others have had occasion, not altogether fairly, to label a blockhead – but there were, of course, the unfathomable tangle of connections within his own consciousness worthy of blame. It was a matter of indifference, or better put, a lack of discernment. Superstitions! Sagredo knew all of them. Every name of every saint, and how he died. Relics and their meanings. Coats of arms and family mottoes. The symbols of witchcraft, the rituals of black magic, the ins and outs of the evil eye – somehow he had passively collected all of this trash and stored it, like some slightly cracked collector of curiosities. It was not unusual to hear him summon up Aleister Crowley in the same breath as Heisenberg.

– Important terrestrials?

– A couple of men difficult to take seriously.

She nodded appreciatively, thinking of a couple of ionic clouds she had been stuck talking to at a party several years back. (Years for her, that is. There will be no use specifying, or even generalizing, about when the party took place; other than to say, that is, that the party certainly does not occur within the period of time in which Myron lived on Earth.)

Myron tilted back the bottle, then continued:

– Best and worst about Sagredo, in the never-quite-final perspective, was that he was a *writer*. Thus, the cheap clothes – go on, admit the connection. This meant that one knew one's work and even one's character were to be stylized and preserved; but this also meant one had to listen, occasionally, to the expression of his anxieties about the "role of the writer" in this or that dire socio-politico-philosophic-historical context. Even Socrates didn't go into so much belabouring of the issues with what's his name, Phaedrus. When Sagredo struck this vein, the only thing for it was to liquor him up and let him gush out all the tautologies he could before he passed out.

He contemplated the bottle, as though it too had just dropped from the sky into his workshop.

– Not much of a drinker, really, given what I hear about writers. His sorest point of contention, though, with all the problems of narrative innovation mumbo-jumbo, drew us together. Do you want to know what he used to say?

She nodded.

– Sagredo used to say that it wasn't Marx or Nietzsche or Freud who shook up how we think and tell stories in this century. It wasn't even Bart or Leotard – I don't know what he was referring to there, but knowing Sagredo, they're probably whacko mystics of some type or another – no, none of them. It was Edwin Hubble, with his space-time connections, which made everything seem so insignificant down here.

– What's a century?

– A hundred years, Myron explained. When the planet orbits the sun one hundred times.

She cocked her head and asked:

– What is the duration of your existence on this planet?

– Well, Myron coughed. He had lost the steam of his oration, and was beginning to dislike this intruder again. Instead of replying, he finished the bottle.

– What was the duration of Sagredo's existence, then?

– Thirty-one, or maybe thirty, er, revolutions.

– Is that a typical duration of existence? she asked.

– No.

Myron rubbed his eye with his thumb.

– He really had such good ears.

– What happened to him?

– He was brutally murdered, came the growling reply. By Simplico.

She nodded, a little sadly but also knowingly, as though this information were to be expected – well, after all, she had heard a rumour that this planet was dominated by a species bent on various forms of self-destruction. Yet as interesting as all this was, she seemed to be drifting away from, rather than toward, the point of her detour. Her thoughts again settled upon the mysterious, beautiful eye.

– I think I have to go now, she said. Nice talking with you.

Myron nodded, more at the empty bottle than at her, and waved goodbye.

At this point in the story we have to change location and go back in time, which is a remarkably easy process in fiction, if nowhere else. To take the story to Padua in 1610, all that needs doing is the insertion of a narrative heading –

Padua

Anno Domini

· 1610 ·

– and here we are, watching another strange man in an altogether different sort of workshop (free of cardboard, for one thing) tinkering with his own invention, and scribbling down his findings in his own bad handwriting. Already he has a title for his intended publication, which he likes to mutter to himself and smile: *Sidereus Nuncius*. It has a smooth feel to it. (Try it yourself: *Sidereus Nuncius*. Nice, isn't it?) The publication of *Sidereus Nuncius* is likely, as one of his friends might put it, to shake loose some thoughts from those on high; but this is of no great concern to him. What matters is the work.

(Incidentally, the story has changed tense. This is to give you a better idea of how close the past actually is; or it helps the narrative seem to give you a better idea how close the past might be.)

"What matters is the work": the phrase reeks of perversion, of obsession. For the truth is that every good scientist is inherently a pervert. Were one to ask the moon (that pale virgin who is not given to conversation) for her opinion on this little Italian man's telescopic activities, she would likely blush – and thereby send the apocalypse-watchers into yet another raving frenzy. Or perhaps, given her general austere aloofness, she would pay no heed, and might even get a secret thrill to know someone so closely and so regularly watched her dance.

The truth is thus; the truth is that Galileo was a peeper.

Or *is* a peeper.

At any rate.

A knock at the door, which he ignores. Another, louder knock, and audible grumbling. Galileo takes his eye (very possibly blue) away from the lens with the twitch of recognition, and proceeds to open the door. His friend looks at him with some emotion poorly disguised as boredom, and they greet each other shortly. Relations have cooled, since that unexpected division of opinion over the sketched blueprint Galileo had made.

– And you propose to build this?

– Propose? said Galileo. I am building it. Nearly finished, in fact.

– I mean, and then are you going to use it?

Galileo permitted himself to smile, but was unable to go on.

– I have warned you before, my friend. You must not go too far. Remember Icarus.

The smile shrank slightly.

– Why is it that warnings from Christians always rely upon earlier myths?

– You are not calling the teachings of Our Lord a myth, surely, dear Galileo. The friend had taken up the remains of Galileo's smile for his own face.

Now (or at least, not then and there) neither of the men are smiling.

– How proceeds your work?

With a pause, Galileo shrugs, relaxes.

– I am, I think, nearly ready to publish.

– You are...you have been looking into the heavens, even when I came? his friend chuckled nervously. Well, carry on. Please do not let me interrupt.

He walks around the room, hands together behind his back and head bobbing, as though he is counting the great number of papers which cover almost every available surface.

– Something is on your mind, says Galileo.

– Yes, yes.

– Please do not have me fish out of you things I do not truly care to hear. What have you come to say? Please say it quickly.

His friend halts in front of him.

– Theology, my friend, is not a subject which interests you, I know. But do you know, Galileo, it has never been the heretics and the mystics who most threaten the Faith. It hasn't even been the more renegade intellectuals or the dirty writers – no, none of them. It was Copernicus, this man I know whom you study, with his blasphemy parading as science, which made everything seem so disordered and imperfect. In the name of science, I tell you.

– I know what Copernicus says, I have read...

– Do you know he was raised a Catholic? That a good Catholic family paid for his education? And that he saw visions of the sun, as hot as the seat which is now his in fiery damnation? In the name of science! And a foreigner, too – he was a foreigner.

Galileo does not look at his friend. He is thinking of what he saw in the sky a few minutes before – but could not have seen. He insists to his visitor that he is too tired to discuss the subject (perhaps another time), and sees him out. Closing the door with his hand to his weary eyes, he breathes a quiet sigh to himself.

– Alas, poor Sagredo!

In the meantime:

Myron will seal himself within his box, and the universe will change. The lonely will still look for love in the eyes of strangers, the truths of the persecuted will have their day, and stories will yet be told. Not necessarily in that order.

A country called Roughage

Pork chops meant applesauce, and the ways each of them pulled their chairs expressed their satisfaction with that equation, part of the harmony she enjoyed, the neatness of having them there together at once and in time for the news. But some of the reports had in recent months stirred the attention of the littlest and explanations however roundabout were becoming part of the fare. And also of some satisfaction was the cleanliness of the kitchen, unusual before the meal and especially during a day when she's been doing the long shift at circulation, clean except for the crumbs under the toaster which, although no one else would give them notice, could not help but seize hers.

– Applesauce yes!

Such signs of delight would make it easier to break the news. Easier for her, she knew she meant, but even so it was not so difficult, not so difficult as it might have been, or not so difficult as she might have wanted. Now what did she mean by having thoughts like that? Applesauce yes indeed. She might take a page out of Rory's book this once.

– Can I help with anything?

She shook her head and took his plate. Arthur always asked this and always asked it too late, actually already seated most of the time. He was a considerate man but not very timely in his consideration, yet this was a quality she'd grown to adore in him, the way he could offer the most unexpected gift at the worst possible moment or how he remembered to thank someone for some great kindness a whole week after the fact.

– Ginny, did you wash your hands?

– Not yet but I was goin to.

– Remember to go easy on the horseradish, Arthur, your stomach.

– Let's turn on the news here.

– No let's, said Lynn, let's let it be, tonight, just be together and we can watch the news on television later.

Probably because there was applesauce there was no debate. Ginny returned from the washroom and held up her open palms to reveal the result, with approving reviews from both parents, cynical brother Rory abstaining.

Lynn joined them at the table after one false start, when she remembered the margarine. By way of ignoring it the kids had positioned the bowl of peas at her end of the table, and after taking her own and remorsefully observing that they looked to be a little overcooked, pushed the bowl back to the centre with a look of instruction.

– I can't get hold of Andy, do you know that?

– Then how can you know if tomorrow's game is on or not? Can you call anyone else?

– Oh, he said and after a pause slowly went on: oh, probably.

She could tell, even though he tried not to show it, that Arthur could tell that something wasn't right and that between his bites he was wondering when, how, if to inquire. The weekly men's volleyball was a subject he only brought up when he could find nothing else with which to fill a silence he detected was awkward. Then he asked:

– How's the library?

She sipped her water.

– Ginny use your fork. Well, Mrs. Aaronow is still in hospital, so we all signed a card today, even some of the after school readers club signed it, but it might be cancer, they don't know yet. And they're all worried about a computer virus but I don't understand half the things they say.

– It's not hard, Mom, I told you all about that.

– Yes, I get some of it Rory but the technician they brought in mumbles and it's bad enough I don't understand. But the withdrawals are nearly done and Des told everybody the budget plan has been drafted.

She blinked and looked at her plate and said:

– Anyway, they decided they won't need me this summer.

– Oh, hon, I'm sorry.

– Well, maybe I deserved it.

– No, don't be ridiculous. He paused, his fork's prongs buried in applesauce. You can't think that way, you know, you're being ridiculous. Times are tight, especially for something the city considers as frivolous as a public library.

She looked away so as not let show how sweetly this balm registered, or was it how little she felt about it, and saw again the crumbs under the toaster.

– What they call downsizing. It's never fair.

– No, said Lynn. She looked at Ginny, who was tracing unusual shapes through the slush she had made of her plate, unable to tell how much of this information was being absorbed. The two of them would have more time together, did she think of that? Ginny looked at her but did not stop stirring. Finally, perhaps realizing she was expected to contribute something, she said:

– It's okay. I don't like being inside in the library for so long.

A snort from Rory, not himself fond of having to drop by to meet his mother in a building his friends had outgrown.

– And I don't like Mrs. Parson, she talks so loud all the time.

– I know you don't but we have to be nice to her, she's very old. Lynn refilled the child's glass of water unasked, and changed tack: You're an outdoor kind of girl, after adventure, well we can do that together. Who do you play with outside now?

– The fairies.

Her father's eyes dropped onto her, a messy mix of amusement and concern in them.

– Fairies?

– Little fairy people. Today in the backyard I caught one of them.

Rory rolled his brown eyes and told them about a geography project, actually something interesting for a change. His parents did not press the subject because they were too pleased to hear of his discovering something scholastic to be enthusiastic about and if there was one rule of parenting they liked to joke about, it was don't push your luck. So unchallenged, Rory went on to say that he was supposed to describe the perfect country, explaining where in the world it would be located, how big it would be, and how many people would live there, how the economy would be sustained, and anything else he might think was important for prospective visitors to know.

– What's the name of your country going to be?

He shrugged, said he was still thinking about it, and asked to be excused. Lynn suddenly remembered a phrase she had read, the day before was it, in a magazine article on the virtues of greens to the diet of both young and old alike. Roughage cleanses the system, that's what it said. As Arthur gave his nod to the two children anxious to escape she thought of saying, what about a country called Roughage, but kept her tongue and watched her daughter run.

Ginny ran away from the peas. Up the stairs, bounding and counting, eleven, twelve, thirteen, thump, she was off to her room of fleecy colours and at the door to her dollhouse made by hand for her by Grandfather Whyte when she was just a baby. Lifting up the roof with a contained smile, she peered inside and with her right hand reached down to the bedroom where her captive fretted, tossing worried blobs of light against the walls, bed, and dresser with moveable drawers. The colours! They were not as pretty and bright as they had been outside but they were still impressive. Ginny sat back in her rocker with her fingers tightly around the fairy and despite its nearly inaudibly tiny screams, she put out both its eyes with a safety pin.

Privileged Motions

— First let me express my sincere hope that all of the, ah, unpleasantness of yesterday's session has dissipated, that we have all cooled down as it were, and that today's session will be considerably more constructive. I know that all of us here appreciate the gravity of the situation as well as the expectations upon us to make some clear, ah, headway in this inquiry. Probably none of us need be reminded of our responsibilities, and I do hope, Mr. Glockenspiel, that you'll find that you share that feeling.

– I'm sorry, what feeling?

– Yes, Mr. Glockenspiel?

– You want me to share a feeling. What feeling were you referring to?

– I just meant, Mr. Glockenspiel, that I hope you appreciate, as we all here should appreciate, the significance of these proceedings, and that today we may overcome the, ah, difficulties of yesterday and make some headway.

– The feeling of appreciation, is that the feeling?

– Mr. Chairman, are we already to start indulging these games with semantics? Mr. Glockenspiel is baiting us again.

– Now, Gary, that's just what I mean, let's try to be patient this morning, no flying off the...

– I just don't get the feeling. That's all.

– And I'm asking for your patience this morning, too, Mr. Glockenspiel.

– Oh, I'm patient, though that's not a feeling either. Appreciation and patience aren't feelings. Fear is a feeling and

I am familiar with it. Joy less so, I'm afraid. But fear is certainly a feeling.

– Here we go again. This is exactly the kind of wind that blew us so far off course yesterday, Mr. Chairman, and in the interest of formality I would appreciate it if you did not use my first name during these proceedings.

– All right, all right, but let's get back to a serious line of discussion. Now yesterday you were posing some questions, Ms. Rossi, and I assume that you would like to continue, or, ah, resume.

– Thank you, Mr. Chairman. Mr. Glockenspiel, I'd like to go back to an answer you gave yesterday before, as Mr. Dunlop has put it, we were blown off course. Yesterday you'll remember I asked you what possible value the colour blue has, and after some evasion on your part...

– There was no evasion. I asked for clarification.

– Yes, yes, you wasted much time establishing what blue was and that provided the stenographers and recorders with some entertainment. Today, however...

– No, that's not correct. I mean, that part about entertaining the stenographers I don't know about, only they can say whether they were entertained, and I doubt whether entertained is truly a feeling, either. But we did not actually establish what blue was or is.

– Mr. Glockenspiel, we appreciate your dedication to a true and accurate record, but I must ask you to let Ms. Rossi formulate her questions and when she has put them to you, I assure you that you will be given ample opportunity to respond.

– Thank you, Mr. Chairman. As we set about trying to establish the nature of blue, Mr. Glockenspiel, if you will allow me to put it in those terms, you seemed to digress from that subject and said, and here I am quoting from the record, "despite your inquiry's preoccupations with the spectral variations of light, the sound of gravity, the best kinds of sewer system, and the absolutely biggest thing in the universe, the fact remains that life has no meaning." Now, since you seem so fixated on this notion which you seem to imply this board of inquiry has not addressed directly...

– Ms. Rossi.

– Yes, Mr. Chairman. I understood that I would be given as ample an opportunity to formulate my question as Mr. Glockenspiel would have to respond, and I am in the midst of formulating my question.

– Ms. Rossi, I am concerned that you are about to steer this vessel right back into the maelstrom of yesterday, if I am not, ah, altogether wearing out Gary's sailing metaphor. Mr. Glockenspiel has, it must be admitted, very patiently allowed the past few weeks of questioning and we have explained to him, again and again, so often that he must be tired of hearing it, that our inquiry's mandate calls for a full and thorough investigation, and that this means an examination of each and every piece of evidence and argument relevant to...

– I appreciate that, Mr. Chairman.

– Mr. Chairman, I'm leaning to Ms. Rossi's side on this one and think she ought to be allowed to finish formulating her question before you barge in with your cautions and concerns.

– Thank you, Mr. Dunlop. My question...

– And I'd like to add for the record that I appreciate your respect, Ms. Rossi, for the formalities of this very important hearing, formalities which I'm sad to see the chair continues to neglect. I would like to repeat for the record my request that I be addressed and referred to properly, in a proper manner befitting this formal inquiry. Everyone else on this board of inquiry manages to observe the proper formalities.

– All right, Mr. Dunlop. Your point is taken.

– I have not taken the point.

– I'm sorry, Mr. Glockenspiel? Did you say something?

– I said I have not taken the point. What is the point?

– And, Mr. Chairman, my point extends very readily to

Mr. Glockenspiel, who has been very patient as you say because contempt can afford to be patient, but let me assure this board of inquiry that when my turn for directing questions comes...

– When it comes, it will then be your turn to direct questions, Mr. Dunlop, but at the moment Ms. Rossi has that privilege.

– Mr. Chairman.

– Yes? Mr. Hacker.

– Mr. Chairman, as you know I have sat silently here the past few sessions, abstaining even from the shouting matches of two days ago and yesterday's free-for-all, even when Ms. Rossi and Mr. Ludd-Erickson made some rather unkind suggestions about the inferiority of green, though both of them know perfectly well my preference for green. As I say you know I have kept my temper and tried to observe these proceedings with a cool and level head, and should like to continue to do so. However, and I hope Ms. Rossi will forgive me if I delay her question just a few moments while I make this position clear, I remain frustrated that no one has probed on even the most superficial level what political allegiances Mr. Glockenspiel professes to hold. He comes before us to discuss this claim, nobody would deny it's anything other than earth-shaking, "life has no meaning," and we don't bother to ask what sort of political background he has. I doubt I am alone in wondering about this.

– Mr. Hacker, your discretion and tact have ever been appreciated here, as I hope are these concerns you raise, which in due course you will have leisure to study. For now, can we agree to acknowledge your concern for the record and allow Ms. Rossi to proceed with her line of questioning?

– Thank you, Mr. Chairman, and may I say that Mr. Hacker should not have taken any comments about green to be at all hostile. I would characterize my own feelings about that colour, with which I have many happy associations, to be more on the neutral side. Now, Mr. Glockenspiel, you use the word "despite" in the quotation I just quoted...

– In what quotation?

– I just quoted you. You said that.

– I said what?

– Yesterday, you said, "despite your inquiry's preoccupations with the spectral variations of light..." and so on. I am wondering why you use the word "despite." That strikes me as a belligerent usage. Could you tell us, please, how you feel about this inquiry? Does all this seem beneath you?

– How I feel? Is that what you're asking?

– Mr. Glockenspiel, I'm asking you to articulate your attitude towards this board of inquiry.

– Attitude.

– How you feel, how you honestly feel.

– Mr. Chairman, I hardly see the point of this question.

– Ms. Linnell, you have an objection?

– Ms. Rossi is asking Mr. Glockenspiel how he feels, I mean I ask you. I can't count how many boards of inquiry I've served on, three or four of them more frustrating than this, how many days have we been here, and even in the most serious ones, you know, nobody asked the witness how he felt, I mean I ask you.

– Mr. Glockenspiel, I'll ask you, do you feel that Ms. Rossi's question is unfair or irrelevant?

– Her question about how I feel?

– Yes.

– Well, it's hard to say.

– Why is it hard to say?

– We started off this session with you suggesting I should be feeling something, sharing a feeling, we never got that straightened out. And now I'm being asked how I feel. It's kind of a trick question, so in that sense I suppose it is unfair. But given that life has no meaning, absolutely no meaning at all, and the question and whatever answer I might give are just parts of life, fair and unfair are categories beyond comprehensible discussion. The same goes for irrelevancy, unless you take irrelevant to be a synonym for meaningless, but that's a bit like equating attitude with feeling.

– There, Mr. Chairman, there's what I'm talking about. A defensive posture. Another evasion. What are you hiding, I wonder, Mr. Glockenspiel?

– I'm not aware of hiding anything. Maybe I am, though, out of fear.

– Are you afraid, Mr. Glockenspiel?

– Really, Mr. Chairman, Mr. Glockenspiel doesn't look afraid and I am worried that Ms. Rossi will go on to inquire if he is sad, if he is mad, if he is glad, and so on and so on and so on.

– Mr. Chairman, may I respond? Look, Paula, you're starting to tire me. Yesterday you interrupted my questions no less than seven times. We have a very serious mandate here and unlike some of the boards of inquiry you've been on, this one has a lot riding on it. We have a mandate, like Stuart said from the top, to investigate the claim that Mr. Glockenspiel here has made, a very serious claim, and I'm asking him if he's afraid. He's said that fear is a feeling, we agree on that?

– Fear is a feeling.

– No, I'm sorry, Mr. Glockenspiel, I wasn't talking to...

– Mr. Chairman, it pains me to see Ms. Rossi surrendering the dedication to formality I praised her for only...

– You're right, Mr. Dunlop, now you see what I've been saying, I mean I ask you, who talks like that on a board of inquiry? I have more respect for this board of inquiry than Ms. Rossi is showing right now and I'd like to remind the board that I did remark from the very first day of this inquiry that Ms. Rossi's commitment to professionalism here was a little dubious, what she was wearing you'll remember was not exactly appropriate to a board of inquiry and I make allowances for differences of fashion.

– All right, all right, that's enough of that...

– Mr. Chairman, maybe I ought to be asking Paula whether she's feeling fear, she seems to think she is the subject of this inquiry!

– Ms. Rossi, please continue, or resume...

– Mr. Chairman, perhaps a break is in order.

– Mr. Ludd-Erickson?

– I said maybe we should take a fucking break.

– Mr. Chairman, I seriously protest. For the record, can you please censure both the inappropriate use of first names by Ms. Rossi and the gross language of Mr. Ludd-Erickson?

– Mr. Chairman, I second Mr. Dunlop's protest, for the record, too.

– Fine, fine, protests noted and suggestion taken. This inquiry will break for one hour. When we come back, I want more, ah, headway, do you understand?

Caught in the Act

By Tuesday I had narrowed the list to eight, and most of them had more or less vivid faces. Nora Hellsen, for instance, had a pert grin beneath her little nose, with lifelong glasses gradually sliding to its little point, while the creature known as Tina Forrester advanced through hallways and open doors with an awareness of what she probably called a developed front, given to wearing sweaters, likely to laugh a little too long at men's jokes. The names spoke to me in different voices, just as accusatory objects and complicit items of furniture were anything but silent themselves: the coffee table, the washroom handtowel, the corkscrew all contained confessions.

And his filing cabinet. At first I was surprised to find it unlocked, and then irritated, as though this were a gesture of flagrancy – *look at how elatedly careless I may be, because of how foolishly trusting you are* – but when my hands fell into the prominent folder marked 262, the course number, my concentration was fully consumed by the names. Wretchedly I memorized all of them, just over sixty in total, including the ones whose sex was not guessable (Jesse McGovern, Shannon Wiley), and most of their grades, too, for good measure. Deena Gutman, who was not one of the ultimate eight but who drew my suspicion at first, looked to be noticeably improving from one assignment to the next, and because I had the spontaneous, admittedly irrational fancy that she had long red hair, she became one of the original prime suspects. *Well, professor, when you put it like that, I suppose you* could *say my attention wanders a little, but it's not that I'm not really interested, it's just*. But when I finally managed to get a glimpse of her, her wiry black hair and coarse habit of waving her hands all the time, as though endlessly washing wide, invisible windows as she talked, convinced me to discard her.

The conference checked out, but when I found myself contemplating an international call to the hotel where he was supposed to be staying, *just calling to confirm the reservation for Professor Reilly*, and heard the sound of my own voice being imagined, not as it really was but as though I were someone else, and worse, someone else playing at being yet another person – well, that's when I did cry. Whoever said tears burn was crazy; you will not catch fire by having a bout of weeping, but you could drown.

I did not drown. Instead of calling the hotel, I tried the campus, reasoning that with the semester in full swing it might not be feasible for a student to up and catch a plane out of the country for a week or more.

Philosophy department, came the secretary's voice.

I asked for Patrick and was told he was on leave.

Yes, I know he's on leave, I said, but I wondered whether he might have dropped by his office today.

No, she said, he's actually out of the country these days.

Her placid voice reminded me, for some reason, of a very plain-looking woman I used to see from time to time in public places. Passing on the street, holding the door at this or that store for the other, we would exchange brief greetings that seemed to confuse both of us: it seemed then, as it seems to me now, that we didn't really know one another, at least we certainly didn't know each other's names and probably could not recall where we had met, but a bizarre sense of obligation initiated these trite interludes. *It's a hot one today isn't it* or *they serve a very nice lunch there for the price* or *it's always something* or *you're looking full of colour* or *you hardly see robins around anymore* or whatever else, none of it memorable and I would produce as much of this stuff as she would. Does it count as a friendship if you do all the things friends do but aren't friends?

Would you like to leave a message? asked the philosophy department's secretary.

No, it's just his wife calling.

Oh, she said, you mean, I mean I didn't know he was married.

For a count of six, seven, eight, I held my breath and then said I would try again later, when the receiver slipped from my hand and bounced against the rim of my half-empty wineglass. Only when the single sound of a double slap against my palms came to me did I understand that my hands had shot out in opposite directions and intercepted both falling objects. Great reflexes, I said aloud, and made another noise, an aborted laugh or a choked sob, killed too prematurely for me to be sure which.

At our wedding, a lavish affair, it seemed impossible not to be galvanized, as though there were some fantastic charge firing through the pews and touching each person in turn. Formerly estranged family members and embittered friends came together and differences were dazzlingly negated – even my mother, rarely disposed to anything other than sour grapes, freely indulged in the wine of gaiety, not to mention the literal variety. Dear, I'm so happy, so proud, she burbled, in a voice that was new to me. Her hand stroked my hair around my ears. So proud, so very happy. Being more accustomed to stony disapprobation, I was left with only weak nods with which to reply. But the strangest, most powerful incident was just as unforeseen. Patrick's father, one of those people who owns six cameras and takes ten minutes to focus on any irritated subject, was leaning awkwardly to capture the thousandth definitive (allegedly candid) moment at our reception when his elbow tipped over a wineglass, and both Patrick's and my hand shot out and caught it together. Great reflexes, everybody said. It became a mantra at the reception but more than that the instant of seizing together the glass became between us a fixture, a totemic sort of gesture, a sign of our own simultaneity. Great reflexes, that was us.

Sometimes I think people have to ask themselves which they really want more: to be sad or to be happy. What I mean is that most people *think* they want to be happy, of course, but so many of them enjoy being distraught; there's a perverse pleasure there that's really popular. Patrick makes me want to be happy. When he's around or I see him or think of him, that perverse pleasure, to which I admit I'm as susceptible as anybody else, is cancelled, replaced with a devotion to joy. I want to be happy, but it has to be said that between the two desires I'm talking about this is the rougher, uphill road. There's no end of material for despair: depression is an omnivore and scavenger, where happiness is a gourmet – or at least fussy.

Like I said, though, I didn't drown in tears. I pursued happiness, a good verb for the activity. Sometimes the pursuit takes place at night, like it did yesterday. Even without daylight exposing its complexion, the Humanities Building is a dreary brick affair, like an ambitious retirement home, I once overheard Patrick describe it. Somnambulant students wandered through its ground floor, irradiating themselves at computer terminals with their very due assignments, but had no reason to take the stairs up to the darkened departmental offices. I can't remember exactly where or when in my life I learned to pick locks – in the course of tomboy childhood, probably, with a stupid grin and nimble fingers – but the confidence with which I approached the office door turned out to be unnecessary: it was not only open, it was ajar. *Leave it, it's more exciting this way*. Even doorknobs have the power to insult my goodwill.

The noises were there, though, and for the first time I was afraid. It is one thing to be gripped by suspicion, for there's a kind of safety in the abstract. It is something else to have real sensory confirmation, to hear as I was now hearing the rustles, the thumps, the breathing. Only half an arm's length away was the light switch, but I hesitated, wondered whether my silhouette was perceptible in front of the invading fluorescent light of the hallway. And there was a thunderous guessing game in those moments of listening in the dark. Was it Tina? Smiling Nora? That slut of a secretary, *I mean I didn't know he was married?* Deena Gutman, even, *oh that feels good professor* while idiotically waving her hands as in front of her? Paired giggles came from the blackness. The next instant the room's lights buzzed weakly and flashed, haltingly, to life. My wrist, startled by its own snap, fell, and my hands were hanging at my sides when I took in the scene.

He was in his fifties, I guessed, but with a tired look to his figure. His exposed buttocks had a kind of plaintive look to them, and the rush to cover them implied a sense of shame about the piteousness they baldly expressed. His face was hard and it was these rigid cheeks, only these, that he showed to the students of his economics seminars, to the fellow members of the professional ethics committee, to the bank tellers and weekly squash partner. Vulnerability and embarrassment were his at that moment – I partook of neither of them, but instead felt something very like disappointment. This stout man grasping at his khakis, with his little ears and fat fingers, was not Patrick. That was all I saw when the lights came on.

Gradually he began talking, but only in short bursts, with an uncertainty about what tone to take the only connection between them. During one of the pauses between bursts, at which I had begun to turn away, a young but sharp voice piped in: That your wife? As I left I absently switched the lights off again, and heard the professor of economics try to explain something about just borrowing the office before the student repeated: Was that your wife?

I was unlocking my bike when he found me. This time his trousers were up and he had settled on an approach. Married, tenured, respectable – he confessed all these things

— 159 —

like adolescent sins – and there was no harm meant, just human pleasure, human weakness. Because I had seen his remorseful rump, his eyes pleaded all the while he spoke, I was the master of the situation.

What about Patrick Reilly? I asked.

He stopped and looked confused, like a pet confronted with an unfamiliar command.

When does he use the office for (my voice quavered) human pleasure, human weakness?

His confusion remained. You mean with a student? I mean, I mean I don't do this all the time! It's just, no harm was meant.

I don't care about you, I hissed, now atop my bike. I'm asking about Patrick Reilly.

I don't know about Patrick, he faltered, I don't know. I mean, I didn't even know he was – I mean, I don't know.

Maybe he said more, but I was pedalling through the parking lot, fury turning the wheels.

Today is Friday, and I have a hangover that has settled in for a weekend together. When I arrived home just before midnight, I did not falter in my actions. Right after I restored the previous order to Patrick's filing cabinet and desk, I popped a disc into the player with the word Repeat illuminated on the display, moved to my five-year-old couch and opened a six-year-old bottle of scotch. *Norma* is the greatest opera for the lost. It is also Patrick's favourite. Three whole times it played, I *think*, before I passed out without once, I *know*, having cried.

Work telephoned just after eleven this morning, and this time I was so sick I did not have the presence of mind to wonder whether I sounded authentically sick. *Norma* was still going and had to be silenced. Sunlight peered through the defective blinds like a relative offering unwanted sympathy. Breakfast was an orange, which came back up more or less entire within the hour. With regurgitated pulp still on my teeth, I telephoned the philosophy department and called the secretary a whore, though it may not have been the same secretary I spoke to a few days ago. Then I looked up the name Hellsen in the telephone book but set the receiver down before I finished dialling. I still did not cry, but brushed my teeth violently enough to make the gums bleed. Then I sat down by the window.

And here I sit. The evening is coming, the conference was supposed to have finished yesterday. In the pane there is a golden reflection, perhaps a little flattering, of a woman who could not be said to be ugly, or even plain. She does look tired, though strong, and it is the strength I admire most about this sunlit ghost. She can endure, I see, for happiness. The wretch in the bathroom mirror with citric saliva running down her chin was despair. I do not want to be that woman. I want to be this patient, glowing twin facing me, seated, wakeful.

Into this likeness slides another image, one of a different tangibility. A taxi has pulled up in front of the apartment complex and the lid of its trunk yawns. After a moment, a backseat door opens and a familiar shoe – a shoe I have held in my hand – touches the curb. My heart, my heart, oh I am standing but barely still. I refuse to be seen at the window, expectant. To be patient does not entail being forlorn, expectant, ridiculous. To be forgiving, if necessary, does not mean surrendering one's dignity. I move away from the window and count but am inconsistent in the measure, the pace haphazard. Imagining the weight of the suitcase in his hand and the effect on his amble up the front steps, I am moving to and from the door, my exhalations against it bounce back warm against my face. There is the front door, the muted tread upon the carpet, and – I open the door.

Hi!

Hello, he says, not quite past. Nice timing.

Have a good trip?

Not bad, he laughs, but you can get tired of spending a whole week with self-important academics.

Bring me any souvenirs?

He laughs again and sets his case down when he reaches number five. Actually, he says, I do have a pretty nice bottle of wine for you – the least I could do – but it's packed away. Right now I really need to crash.

There is exhaustion in his movements when he unlocks the door and steps inside, comes back out for his case.

Professor Reilly! I toss his spare keys to him and almost without looking he throws out a hand and seizes them from the air. Great reflexes, I call.

Patrick, he smiles, and his apartment door closes behind him.

My hands are pressed tightly together, and when I close my own door the disarray of the room strikes me forcefully. What a fool, what a fool. My faith must be somewhere under all this mess, and it will need to be polished. I empty the remains of the scotch down the sink and set the bottle amid the recyclables. I return *Norma* to its case. I scrub and see a tear hit the stove.

He's come back.

Loss of an Icon

The bonfires, some half-dozen of them, were already blazing by the time I arrived. The route had been treacherous and when I asked a gaunt, loping man if the direction I was taking was right, his eyes rolled about in their sockets and his hands clutched at his tie as though he were trying to strangle himself by degrees. Then I knew I was close, but this was a very mild taste of the lunacy I was about to witness.

Last Friday night was the funeral of Stuart McLean, but if I had expected a hero's send-off or a somber farewell to a distinguished man of letters, the reality that awaited me in that muddy field far from the city lights enjoyed the power to surprise.

There were many, many people – there was no way to count, but I seldom saw the same face or figure twice – and given the noise, conversation was nearly impossible. At one point I did manage to ask a woman of about fifty, who had swerved into me with her arms in the air, which of McLean's titles meant the most to her. I had to repeat the question because she was preoccupied with smearing a plum across her mouth.

"*Welcome Home*, perhaps?" I offered. "Or do you prefer the radio broadcasts?"

She described an unnatural act she had always wanted to try. When I tried to change the subject, she became violent. It had been a mistake, it seems, to assume that because she was wearing most of her clothes, she was not subject to the deluge of grieving madness that held the hundreds of people rolling about in the muck, bawling obscenities, by turns beating each other and copulating furiously, devouring piles of fruit and vegetables (many of which were clearly rotten and with worms), wandering about in a daze. The woman with whom I'd been conversing abandoned us to throw up on a nearby dwarf or child who was half-singing, half-humming while masturbating and whose voice never broke as the slop hit him square in the face. I would have felt nausea then if it had not been for the couple behind me who were violently squeezing my buttocks and smacking their lips.

Some of the fights were very serious, and when I first tried to make my escape, keeping my head low and muttering the words "vinyl café, my favourite, vinyl café" like a mantra to protect me, I stumbled across a severed forearm on which was tattooed the name MORLEY over a heart jaggedly broken in two. My own scream was killed by another, the combined effort of a pair engaged in a twirling embrace, whether dance or headlock, impossible to say, which had taken them into and through one of the tall fires. I recognized one of them as a CBC technician I had once met at a party: at that time he had seemed quite reserved. He doused himself in the mud and collapsed, but a fellow mourner with a cane began prodding him and cursing him in gutter French.

When I realized – or rather surrendered to the realization – that there was no way through the crowd without being torn to pieces, that any sanity would be identified as a lack of respect for the deceased, I removed my shirt in what I hoped was a sufficiently savage manner and emitted a low growl. Immediately a pregnant woman attached her mouth to my nipples and begged me to tell her the stories were not gone, they could not be finished.

"They will go on," I said, but yelped the last word when she bit down very hard. I was bleeding, the areola dangled, but all I felt was exaltation. I was bleeding for Stuart. This was what was needed. I knocked the pregnant woman into a puddle and hollered at the sky, a wild and great sound, and felt the heat of the fires close. The records were spinning. The stories endured. I was eating a stranger's excrement, watching an idealistic young man pull out his hair in handfuls, chuckling as he walked in ellipses. Stuart was gone. The universe, the world, held, with all its quirks and unexpected moments, remained. The stories would go on.

Reader, we buried him.

Last One In

Have I mentioned that I have an extraordinary sense of hearing? It's really something. You know how some people complain that they can hear their neighbours talking – you know, right through the walls. They say that they can hear them gabbing on the phone, and some people even say that they can hear the voice of the other person on the phone, the person talking to the neighbour, the person who is not next door at all. Well, I tell those people, that's nothing. When my neighbours are watching a movie on television, I can hear every word. That's supposed to be extraordinary? asks Frederic. And when a character in the movie my neighbours are watching answers a telephone call, I can hear every word spoken by the voice of the other person on the phone, even if the person perhaps doesn't appear in the movie at all. That, I conclude, is extraordinary hearing.

Frederic says I exaggerate but Camille is amused. There may be some pleasure to be had in deluding oneself, says Frederic, but the physical senses were made for the physical world and I, for one, am a physical being, not one who lapses readily into feeble fantasy. You can boast all you like about things which cannot be proven. I, for my part, prefer tangible accomplishment to vague quality. Since you mention hearing, let me demonstrate with an example on just that score. As it happens, several friends and acquaintances have remarked more than once upon my own extraordinary sense of hearing. If you will permit one moment of silence (*which we do*), I can declare without fear of contradiction that, in the moment of silence that has just passed, someone in the apartment three floors directly above us opened a can using a manual opener. Do either of you doubt the accuracy of this report?

I suggest we follow through with our friend's suggestion, despite the inconvenience such theatrics on his part pose, not simply because we were all of us rather comfortable but because the building's only elevator is out of service and we shall have to take the stairs (*which we do*).

Please excuse our intruding, Frederic warbles to the weary-looking septuagenarian who answers the door of the apartment in question. My friends here and I were just now having a discussion about hearing, and to display my own extraordinary sense of hearing I told them I heard someone in your apartment use a can opener a few minutes ago. They don't believe I actually heard such a thing.

There's no soliciting in this building, the septuagenarian says firmly.

Camille is definitely amused.

Frederic waves his hands as though to keep the door open by magic. No, no, he says, I'm not trying to sell you anything. I'm simply asking whether you or someone else in your apartment happened to use a can opener in the past few minutes.

I don't need a can opener, the septuagenarian says even more firmly. I've already got one.

Frederic inhales audibly, perhaps looking for patience from the atmosphere, and tries again. You possess a can opener, that is very good, that is wonderful. Have you used it recently? Did you, or possibly someone else, use it a few moments ago? To open a can, I mean?

There's nobody else in this apartment, comes the answer.

That, I announce with a half-step forward, is a falsehood. In truth of fact you share the premises with three cats, one of them just a little plumper than the others. You see, I explain to the astonished person, they are padding about your carpeted floors altogether too faintly for my friends to discern it, perhaps you yourself are unable to hear them at this moment here in the hall, but I have a rather extraordinary sense of hearing.

Hunh, replies the septuagenarian, who closes the door very firmly indeed.

Camille's amusement is now palpable, can be tasted on the air. Somewhat citrus. I have not fully worked out a comprehensive theory of pheromones but, and here is where I began to put this train of thought onto the rails of speech, it may very well be that, first of all, we human beings express ourselves in aroma as much, as variously, as blatantly or as subtly as the moment requires, as we do in, for example, sounds, including speech. Second, this phenomenon is effectively a conversational one, and our odors are ever responding to each other, with, as my first point suggests, as much complexity and richness of feeling and thought as we use in our other sense-linked forms of communication, such as our body language. However, it is the third hypothesis, if that is not too weighty a word for my thinking out loud, that is the real corker.

Hush! cries Frederic suddenly, his arms spread apart for effect: Do you not hear it?

Your hearing is obviously at fault here, I say as lightly as I can, for we have changed tunes entirely. We have left the auditory realms for the as-yet-undiscovered olfactory ones.

Yes, I hear but pay no attention to these diversionary tactics. I repeat, I am very much a physical man (*with an obvious bending to Camille*) in the physical world, and your abstractions may fill time but not (*with a further bending*) our appetites, our hearts. Nor are they immediate, and what I have perceived is immediate.

Camille asks Frederic to divulge what he has heard that we have not. Obviously I am a little irritated at having the exposition of my third precept concerning pheromonal conversation postponed in this way, because it really is something worth hearing, but one can usually expect the pleasure of observing proud Frederic doing something ridiculous.

It would be impossible not to allow that your sense of the dramatic, at least, is extraordinary, if not your hearing. All right, what do you hear, Frederic?

We must return at once to the apartment above, where the septuagenarian is telephoning the police! There has been a serious misunderstanding. Even now the septuagenarian is calling us solicitors, hoodlums, no-gooders, implying that we must have broken into the building somehow, that we made obscure sales pitches and then threats. Threats even to the cats!

That means taking the stairs again (*which we do, some of us reluctantly*), and though I like exercise as much as anybody, this is a little silly. Frederic says that my complaints must drive Camille crazy, but she does not reply and I don't think she's amused.

On the way up the stairs, we encounter four anxious people coming down. They have just heard a report that someone has broken into the building, that the police are on the way. One of them alludes to a heart condition but another tells the rest of us that this is just a fantasy. A short argument holds us in place between floors. Frederic tries to explain that it is all a misunderstanding, but the anxious person who may have a heart condition takes great offence, thinking that he is referring to the medical argument now under way between all of the anxious people but one, whose heart I can hear going like mad and whom I suspect has a very serious heart condition but is too modest or shy to say anything about it. Frederic's attempts to steer the discussion back to his misunderstanding are fruitless, and when I gently inquire after the health of the quietest and palest of the anxious people, Frederic gives me a look of near-revulsion. I'm fine, says the anxious person in question, surprised by the question. Camille draws everyone's attention to the approaching sound of sirens, and after a moment of listening we all of us resume our respective directions up and down the stairs.

Just as we arrive at the septuagenarian's floor, however, I

pause. Forgive me for my mentioning my remarkable sense of hearing again, I whisper to Camille, but did you hear the heartbeat of that anxious person down there, the quiet one, the one I spoke to? I can hear it still, that heart, and it's going like mad. In fact it's terrifying how fast it's going, and none of those other anxious people going downstairs seems to notice it. That anxious person is about to have some sort of attack, I've got to go and help (*and I do*).

I hear every note of what happens upstairs at the same time that I encounter a detective and two uniformed officers a few floors below. While Frederic is knocking on the septuagenarian's door, I am giving my name to the detective and trying not to act too jumpy or too casual or in any way suspicious. As Frederic pounds harder on the door and says that he is not a solicitor, that there has been a misunderstanding, Camille suggests that the septuagenarian may be too frightened to answer the door, and the detective instructs me to go down to the parking lot with the other anxious people who have left the building. I suddenly divine a decisive way to test Frederic's hearing, and while Frederic announces to the unopened door for the sixth time that there has been a misunderstanding and that he means no harm to the septuagenarian nor to the septuagenarian's cats, I mention to the detective as I go, in as clear a tone as I can manage, that a suspicious-looking character was banging on doors upstairs. The detective halts and asks for a description, which I give (*one of Frederic*), just as Camille says that Frederic is being ridiculous and he should leave off bothering the confused septuagenarian. Within a second of her saying this, the apartment door flies open and the septuagenarian is there screaming, I'm only sixty-five! And as the detective and the uniformed officers race up the stairs toward the scream, the self-confessed sexagenarian unleashes a cougar on poor Frederic.

These are sounds I shall never forget: of the snarling cougar having its way with Frederic, of Camille's screams, of the detective and the uniformed officers repeatedly shooting the cougar, of Frederic choking his last breath through much blood, of the sexagenarian, whose heart it was I heard going mad all that time, dropping dead at the sight of this melee.

And yet I confess that these are not the worst sounds, the sounds which haunt me most. I know even before I re-enter the building with the anxious people that I'm going to move away from this place. I'll have to, since I cannot afford the rent alone. And I know that I'll miss Frederic and our arguments, even though he always tried in vain to outdo me in every little thing. And I know, I'd like to think, that Frederic would want me to have Camille to myself, and together we might remember him from time to time, fondly I mean, when he was ridiculous, not when his throat was torn out by a savage cougar he mistook for an overweight cat. I know, Frederic; I know.

What I do not know is that the detective is not only handsome and brave but amusing, more than amusing, that is Camille's phrase, and she meets him regularly after all of the reports are written and official business done. They move away together and that is the last I see of her, but block my ears though I try, each night I hear perfectly every sigh and turn of their lovemaking, wherever they may be.

Acknowledgments

A number of these fictions have previously appeared (some in slightly different form). They are "Means to an End" and "Loss of an Icon" (*Queen Street Quarterly*), "Constellation" (*3rd bed*), "Way to Go" (*Lilies and Cannonballs Review*), "An Unlikely Sequence" (*Henry Street*), "Good Faith" (*filling Station*), "The Watch" (*The Danforth Review*), "Plot" (*Kiss Machine*), "The Tip" (*paperplates*), "The Annotated Affair" (*Zygote*), and "Solacium" (*Existere*). "In the meantime" was published as a chapbook by In Case of Emergency Press. Thanks to these publications' respective editors.

A few notes which may or may not be helpful. Unlike the South California fiddlehead, the plant mentioned at the end of "The greenhouse effect" is not an invention of the author's. Footnote numbers in "The Annotated Affair" run parallel to specific United Nations resolutions from 1990. "Loss of an Icon" is *après* Apollinaire: Stuart McLean is not, at the time of this writing, clinically dead.

Thanks to Stephen Cain, as good an editor as he is a friend, and to Mike O'Connor of Insomniac Press. Support from the following individuals is appreciated in ways that such a list cannot demonstrate: Steven Heighton, Jason Heroux, Bernard Kelly, Jay MillAr, Gail and Julian Scala. Clelia Scala knows the rest of the book's title.